Wide Plank Porches

A Novel

Laura Frances

Lost Sock Publishing

Wide Plank Porches
Laura Frances

Lost Sock Publishing
Laurinburg, North Carolina 28352

First published in the United States of America by Lost Sock Publishing

Cover design by Laura Polk

ISBN-13: 978-1546454182

ISBN-10: 1546454187

10 9 8 7 6 5 4 3 2 1

www.laurafrancesauthor.com

For Shantel and Michele
Thank you for introducing me to
the One I'd been looking for my entire life.

I'm forever grateful.

Chapter One

Charlotte

According to my sister, Purdy, Mama ushered me into this world with a glass of chardonnay and a wistful sigh. I imagined it was more like a shot of liquor and an all-out hissy fit, if she was as much like me as everyone said. But, the Parkers had an image to protect and it trumped the truth every time.

Taken from me before I could imprint her face into my memory, I never heard Mama's story first hand. Her gentle ways faded into our family history before I had the chance to tell her I was in desperate need of someone like her, someone like me.

Parker women were known for three things: southern graces, storytelling, and sassiness. The second to some, would be called outright lying. The last being something outsiders seemed to find unusual for women with such a gentle upbringing. Outsiders of course, being Northerners—or Yankees rather, if none were in listening range—which all Parkers had been raised to despise, but I had married.

The scent of magnolia and fresh cut grass placed me on alert as I pulled up to the guard gate at the Carolina Country Club. I longed to be in my own garden, planting the summer bulbs that had been delivered earlier in the week—a small remnant of the creative girl I used to be. Instead, I was doing my duty. Giving Purdy the attention she so readily demanded, so she would leave me alone to pursue my dream of opening my own flower shop. A dream I kept hidden from her.

The security guard nodded at me from inside the little window, "Good morning, Mrs. Johnston," and pushed the button to lift the gate for my entry. Beyond the stacked stone walls that rolled from the gate post down to the grass, red buds nudged through their winter hiding spots and filled the trees that lined the drive. Rows of azaleas planted closely together created a blanket of pink and white beneath the trees. The beds then dipped to blue periwinkle flowers, hedged by monkey grass that overflowed to the curb.

The eighteenth green sat to my right, sculpted and bustling with golfers taking their turn at wrapping up a fine morning. A life of ease. One I supposedly shared but longed to be away from. Just the rules of it, of course. I didn't mind the amenities. I turned onto the winding brick drive that followed the slight curve of the fairway, stopping at the valet.

I stepped out of the car and dangled my keys.

"Good day, Mrs. Johnston." Reid Morley winked as he rushed to my side. He took the keys, holding them and my hand for an inappropriately long time. I glanced away. His white loafers were scuffed along the edges, something I'd been trained to note. I hated myself for doing so.

"Did your mama see those baskets I dropped by the house for the garden club?" Surely, all he needed was a reminder that I was his mother's age. He was sixteen for goodness' sake.

"Um. Yes ma'am. She did. Thanks." His face reddened.

I nodded as he let my hand drop. From the front steps, I could hear Purdy's shrill voice cackling with the other women inside. I sighed, then smiled a wide smile and pushed myself forward, into the lion's den.

"Well. Look who decided to show up." Purdy screeched across the room. She sat at the large back table, with a handful of other women. Her graying blonde hair was pulled into a tight bun, making her dour features even more severe than usual. The steel blue Parker eyes narrowed to penetrate me to the core. Purdy made her point then huffed as she turned to the group, resituating the linen napkin on her lap, and pulling down the hem of her Chanel jacket.

I made my way around the exquisitely decorated table, kiss-kissing and apologizing for my tardiness. The smell of expensive perfume mingled with the tantalizing scents of rack of lamb being prepared in the nearby kitchen. The ladies were overdressed as usual considering the club's recent policy of "coat optional." Enough Chanel, Prada, and Versace surrounded that table to start a small boutique. I was fully aware that each one of them prepared for today through painstaking hours—as they did each week. Dressing to perfection was competitive sport to this crowd.

I sat down and turned toward Purdy. "You know, that Mercedes you talked me into isn't the most reliable thing. I swear it almost died its seventh death coming out of the driveway."

All eyes turned to Purdy, gauging her reaction. "Oh, pooh. That thing's the best decision you've made in months. You look just precious driving it through town, Charlotte."

The other women nodded and hummed amongst themselves in agreement as I wondered why on earth my tardiness had been let off the hook. Purdy's gaze diverted to the entrance and I soon realized my reprieve. Maimie Cramer stood at the doorway, a look of reluctance overwhelming her impeccable ensemble. She smiled sweetly as she crossed the room, as if to beg for mercy, and took the last remaining seat—beside Purdy.

"I'm so sorry I'm late, girls," Maimie offered. "It's been the most unusual morning."

"Oh, I should say so." Purdy didn't hesitate to go for the kill. "We've been worried sick about you and your family all week, Maimie. I couldn't stand the wait to see you. How are things coming together after, you know, the news?"

Maimie fidgeted with her purse, moving it to the floor, then to her lap, and back again. "Oh, there's no news, really. Justin and his college roommates got into a silly little mess, but you know how that goes. I'm sure it was blown way out of proportion around here." Maimie's eyes flitted around the table as if to avoid direct eye contact with Purdy.

"Well, now that's not what I heard." Purdy laughed, her gaze sweeping the table with eyebrows raised. "But, it's not really my place to say. I'm just glad I don't have grown children running amuck all over such a fine university campus and ruining my good name. Don't you agree, ladies?"

The women at the table nodded their heads, as if on cue. I searched my mind for a way to change the subject. But, as always happened in moments of extreme awkwardness, my arsenal of small talk was empty.

Maimie straightened herself for the battle, "What, pray tell, did you hear, Purdy?" Her words were simply a dare to someone like my sister.

"I don't think I'd better say." Purdy raised her voice. "I mean, drug overdoses, stolen bank accounts. I wouldn't want to spread any rumors. It's a pathetic turn of fate for such a fine young man, Maimie. How do you even sleep at night, knowing what a wretched waste of time he's been?" Purdy wiped her mouth with her napkin as if satisfied by a meal even though we'd yet to eat.

Maimie's mouth fell open, while the rest of the table sucked in a breath. Purdy had crossed the line.

"Not that it's your fault." Purdy's voice almost sang as she retreated a bit. "Of course not. All children are selfish parasites, just waiting to take advantage of their parent's generosity."

The ladies nodded in agreement like a row of ridiculous bobble head dolls wiggling to the vibration of someone else's movement.

"Some parent's slack just allows them a quicker road than others," Purdy said.

I jerked my head toward Purdy, furious at her little game. I wanted desperately to do something, but didn't know what or how. I always felt so helpless around the Parkers and completely inept—a fact that got on my very last nerve. Why had Maimie come knowing what awaited her? But then again, not coming was often worse and could result in a much deeper wound.

Maimie took the napkin she'd laid in her lap and began refolding it. Some of the ladies had drawn their hands to their mouth in shock, as others watched with a smug smile. I wondered if they'd been thinking—but didn't have the gall to say—the exact words that fell from Purdy's hateful mouth.

I shifted in my seat. "Well, I think it's just a small bump in the road for Justin, Maimie. You know, one of those college things. We've all been there. I'm sure you have it under control."

Purdy's head snapped in my direction. "Oh, you would think so."

My stomach tightened at the judgmental look on Purdy's face. Was the comment meant for Maimie or me? My mind wandered to my own daughter. Janie was finishing her sophomore year and returned home only a few days before for spring break. Had Janie ever been to the types of parties Justin was rumored to frequent? Did Purdy know something?

The waiter hovered around the table, filling water glasses and flirting with the attention-starved wives. Maimie's eyes filled with tears as she lowered her gaze. I prayed she wouldn't give Purdy the satisfaction of crying in front of the group.

Purdy's hand reached across the table, as if a peace offering. "Oh, now. Don't do that. Crying isn't going to make it any better, Darlin'. You've got to buck up and get that boy in line. Besides, I'm sure you're not the only one around here trying to hide something." Purdy's eyes scanned the table, looking for her next victim. They settled for a moment on me, then diverted to the larger group.

Maimie's phone rang, a ring-tone I didn't recognize at first, but decided was one of those praise-and-worship songs. Purdy's lips drew into a tight line, annoyed at the fact that someone arrived at lunch without turning off her cell. A flurry of manicured hands dipped into their purses, double-checking that their ringers were off.

Maimie left the table, and crossed the dining room to the terrace. Purdy rolled her eyes and huffed.

I leaned toward my sister, "Really, Purdy. Do you have to be so obvious? Give her a break. None of us is perfect."

"It's just girl talk, Charlotte. Don't get your panties in a wad. She knew it was coming. It's what we do. I'm just keeping it interesting around this stuffy old place." Purdy winked at the ladies. Which of them would offer herself for sacrifice next week? She turned back to me. "And don't lecture me about perfection. I don't need a lesson in manners from you."

"I swear, if you weren't my sister . . ."

"You'd what? You should thank the good Lord I'm your sister, Charlotte. My goodness, if anyone needs a watch dog, it's you." Purdy flipped a stray hair to the side and laughed.

A snicker from the other side of the table alerted me to the sinister fact that I was being prepped as next week's victim. My mind raced with thoughts of what could be going on. Folding my napkin and placing it on my chair as I stood, I excused myself from the table. Then, instead of heading to the ladies room as I intended, I found myself at the valet stand watching Reid jump the fence border in what seemed a vain attempt to impress as he fetched my Mercedes.

As my door was held open, a couple entered the club for lunch and I could hear Purdy's voice boom from inside, "Well, good gracious. How long does a potty break take?"

I slid into the driver's seat and pushed the pedal to the floor. Glancing in my rear view mirror, I couldn't help but grin at the rubber mark I left along my escape route.

Chapter Two

Janie

I knew it was no biggie, but I couldn't stop pacing my room. Stopping every few feet to scribble my random thoughts on a piece of scrap paper, I knew I had to come up with the right way to tell Mama. Aunt Purdy had already informed me of the Sunday lunch coming up next weekend—as if—and I knew I had to take care of it before then. The least I could do was to make sure Mama knew first. But, it had to be just the right way—and super-fast.

It was risky, coming home with a secret like this in a town where women suspecting anything were like bloodhounds on a bone. Especially Purdy. I had to do it soon, maybe today. Like ripping off a Band-Aid—painful but necessary.

The smell of burning coffee drew me into the kitchen just as it did every morning for as long as I could remember. Mama could be so careless. Steam rose from the glass pot as I filled it full of water and liquid detergent to soak in the sink. It's a wonder the entire thing wasn't black by now. Funny how it was one of the smells that reminded me of home.

Mama's car idling in the driveway earlier that morning was a sure sign she would be occupied with her Monday lunch with the gaggle of hens she called friends. Why she put herself through such torture was beyond me. As I'd watched her drive off, all I could think was that she needed to get a backbone and learn to say no.

A flash of lime green caught my eye as my best friend, Jenn, rode past the house in her Corolla and parked along the street. Living just a few doors down, Purdy would hate seeing such a clunker out in front of the family home, in broad daylight. Not to mention the "devil music" she was blaring as loud as possible. I swear I think Jenn saved that song just for Purdy. I'd never heard her play it anywhere else. I was sure I would hear about it later.

Slipping the ragged piece of paper under my mattress, I pulled the hand-sewn quilt further down on one side so it wouldn't be noticed. I rushed down the back staircase and out onto the slate patio, which led into the garden. An old, crooked swing still hung from the tree house in the back corner near the shed.

Jenn and I spent our lives in my backyard, chasing fireflies, painting fingernails and toenails, and discussing boys. The worn seat on the faded white swing served as a reminder of the many times I'd comforted Jenn over her never-ending family problems. Between her parent's incessant fighting and Jenn's rebellious ways, the environment she lived in was intense. With no siblings, we were as close as sisters. Sisters who were total opposites, that is.

The old oak that witnessed life at the home since the war of Northern aggression—as my Grandpa Parker called it—seemed to lean in to the conversation as we shared. Its sturdy waist and outstretched arms were a comforting reminder of home, grounding me.

"I got here as quick as I could." Jenn's auburn hair blew in wavy lines across her face as she rushed toward the tree house swing. She lifted her hand to push the strands aside and shaded her chestnut colored eyes against the sun.

A weak smile was all I could offer as my stomach churned and I suddenly felt nauseated at the smell of raw fertilizer coming from Mama's gardening shed. The warmth of the spring sun lay on my shoulders but inside I felt chilled. Jenn pulled me into a hug as she sat beside me, then pulled back to search my eyes.

"Are you sure, Janie? You've taken the test and everything? The blue line one? You saw a blue line?" Her eyebrows furrowed.

"Yeah, Jenn. I took the test. Five of them, in fact. Five blue lines. I'm definitely pregnant." I pulled at the peeling white paint chips on the swing's arm.

"Wow. Well. That's good, though. Now you know, right?"

"Yeah, I know. It's good." I was relieved she agreed. I leaned my head on her shoulder. Jenn stroked my hair as I stroked my stomach.

The news wasn't terrible. A possible bad decision on my part, and maybe not the best timing, but I couldn't turn my back on the result. A baby. That was a beautiful thing, right? I was dying for someone else to care about it. Dying for someone to tell me what to do next. Precarious for someone in my circumstance.

"You're going to be fine, Janie. Really. And we can still move to Myrtle Beach this summer. I've already talked to my uncle about getting us jobs. He's fixin' to open another restaurant right on the new boardwalk they're building. This doesn't have to change a thing." Jenn rubbed my back and leaned to touch heads.

My eyes welled up with the relief of having her in my life. "Thanks, Jenn. I knew you'd make me feel normal. I mean, it's not like I'm the first girl my age to have this happen. It's not even a big deal anymore."

"I know, right? I've even heard of a guy you can go to. Someone over in Malton who takes care of these things."

My breath caught in my throat as if I'd been reamed in the middle. Sitting straight up, I pushed Jenn away from me. How could she bring up something like that, knowing all the hours I'd put into the campus Pro-life campaign? She knew how I felt about everything. Especially this.

"Jenn! I could never. I'm not—there is no way I can do something like that. I wasn't raised like that. It's just . . . wrong, Jenn. It's wrong." Tears fell faster than I could control as I stumbled to get off the swing and away from the thought. I wanted to run. But, without Jenn. . . What if my family reacted the same way? I'd be completely alone.

"Janie. You're about to finish your sophomore year at State. You start your internship in the fall. We're moving to Myrtle in, like, two months. You've got your entire life ahead of you. You can't. You just can't. It's not right—for the baby, I mean. You can't be a mother now." Jenn's voice broke and then trailed off as she walked around the tree as if searching for a way to get me to agree.

"Right for the baby. Yeah. You're bubbling over with concern." I wished I'd kept my secret to myself.

"Well, what if . . . what if there's something wrong with it, Janie? What then?"

"What does that mean? Why would there be something wrong with it? Oh. I see where you're going with this. Because I did something 'bad,' I get something bad. Is that it? More of your 'balance of good and evil' bit?"

"Well, it's true, you know. Whether you admit it or not. What goes around comes around. You do something negative, something negative has to happen to you. The universe has to balance out."

"Since when did you see sex as negative? Where's the whole 'it's my body and I can do what I want' attitude? Pregnancies aren't automatically bad, Jenn." Did I know how she truly felt about anything? Maybe all that posturing was for show, as Mama always said.

11

Jenn shrugged and rolled her eyes. "Just because you don't buy into what I believe doesn't make it untrue."

Ditto. I'd been raised in the church. I knew right from wrong. Even if I didn't understand all the rest of it. "And, what about what you're suggesting I do? That isn't bad? This is more than a thing to be taken care of, Jenn. It's a baby. It's my baby." The last words echoed in my ears.

Jenn crossed her arms and widened her stance. She tilted her head looking at me, incredulous. "You're twenty. Do what you want."

"Maybe I'll do what's right." I should've known we'd have opposite opinions.

A board creaking in the tree house above caused my entire body to jerk. I peered upward, panicked.

"I've got to go," Jenn said with tears in her eyes. She hurried across the lawn as I reached for her but missed. I glanced up to see two brown eyes open wide in disbelief, and then shut tight.

Zee was hiding.

* * *

I rushed to the worn ladder rungs Daddy hammered directly into the tree so many years before. Stopping as I caught my finger on the splintered top of the bottom rung, I thought of the many times I'd raced Jenn and Zee to the top. Summer days that felt like weeks.

I took each step with care, making sure the planks still held, and climbed to the first platform: the lookout. It was the last open space before the next level, which was completely enclosed: the hideout. The higher up I moved, the more cramped the space became. Zee snickered as I moved closer and I realized how much I'd missed him. A child still, regardless of the fact that we were the same age.

I crouched at the door and knocked. Six knocks. Two knocks. One knock. Our secret signal. The door creaked open, then closed, then open.

I peeked in to see Zee sitting on the old twin mattress. He held the string mechanism we'd rigged to open the door in one hand, and Bracey, the doll my Grandma Parker made when she was a girl, in the other. Zee rocked the rag doll back and forth, stroking her yellowed fabric face. Both age and pollen had taken their toll on Bracey.

Being with him there, I still felt like a child. Comfortable around the forgotten toys we'd abandoned so many years ago. Sitting among stale stuffed animals and walls covered in bubble gum wrappers. I knew my life would be so different soon.

"Janie's baby." Zee handed Bracey to me. He touched her yarn hair and surveyed her as if he still wanted to hold her, but knew she was mine.

"Did you hear me and Jenn talking, Zee?" I hoped it was over his head. A thought that made me feel terrible, but grateful for the possibility at the same time.

Zee shrugged his shoulders, his brown eyes looking up at me from beneath a layer of thick blond hair that seemed to have a life of its own. He touched Bracey once more.

"Sweet baby." I tried to ease him into telling me if he understood.

"Janie's baby." Zee nodded as he scrutinized the doll, then my stomach.

My eyes burned with tears. I thought of the bad example I was setting for Zee, whose mama was a devout Christian—really living it. "Yes," I said leaning over to kiss the doll's head. "Janie's baby."

"I like babies." Zee smiled and reached for Bracey. He held her and rocked her side to side in his overzealous way, pretending to comfort her. "I take care you baby too. See? I good at it."

"You are, Zee. You're really good at it." I forced myself to give him an encouraging smile. "You're good at keeping secrets too."

"Yeah. I'm good at not telling. I willn't." He pulled his lips inward as they formed a tight line.

"Promise me, Zee. Swear."

"Pomise." He held three fingers up, a throwback to the Brownie troop Jenn and I tried to form when we found out boys weren't allowed, but Zee wanted to be a Brownie. He pretended to turn a key on his lips and flung his hand haphazardly to toss it out the window.

I leaned over to hug him. "You're the best friend I have, Zee. Always have been."

He lowered his head as a wide smile filled his face. He put Bracey back on the bed and covered her up with a torn blanket, peeking to see if I'd noticed. He propped a sun-faded comic book beside her and placed a cup of imaginary milk in her hand. I had to force myself not to cry.

We stood and hunched down, filling the space. Zee rushed ahead, but I was careful to make my way out and turned to peek in once more before closing the door for good.

Zee skittered down the ladder in a way that made me nervous. He'd never taken on the fears growing older instills in you. I stepped carefully, making sure each foot was stable before moving on to the next rung.

As I reached the bottom of the old oak, I found Mama sitting on the swing, gardening tools in hand, eyes wet. My heart constricted.

Zee took one look at Mama and somehow knew to go home.

Mama glimpsed over her shoulder and motioned toward the back of the garden shed. In the far corner of the yard sprawled mounds of spring flowers sorted by type and color. Mama's delicate hands were covered in the dark speckled soil that would become their home. It never crossed my mind she might come home early and work in her garden. Her one stress reliever.

Mama sat in silence, begging me with her blue eyes. The tiny wrinkles that surrounded them when she smiled now just made her look worn.

I knew she heard everything. I knew she wanted me to tell her it wasn't true.

"Mama . . ." I sat beside her and placed my hand over hers as she remained motionless. No reaction. "I wanted to tell you, Mama. I did. I didn't know how."

"Does Drew know?" Her voice wavered, making me tear up.

"Yes," I whispered. I never meant to let her down.

Neither of us moved. No one uttered a sound. I leaned my head on Mama's shoulder and felt her tense up. I was sure she hated me for what I'd done.

"Who else?" Mama whispered in a voice hoarse with restrained emotion.

"Who else, what?" What kind of girl did she think I was? There was only Drew.

"Who else knows, Janie? Is everyone in town talking about us? Do all your friends from high school know? Have you plastered your shame all over town so your family can be as humiliated as possible by your carelessness?"

"Mama, what shame? I didn't—"

"Didn't what, Janie? Didn't think about us? Didn't know how pregnancy happens? Didn't think we would find out? Didn't what? Didn't what!" Mama pushed me off her and stood, staring down at me. I felt so small in that moment.

"I'm sorry, Mama. No one else knows. Except Jenn. And Zee. But I didn't tell him, he overheard."

"Great." Mama let the garden tools fall from her hands and walked shoulder-slumped toward the house.

I fell in step behind her, determined to make her see my side. "It's going to be okay, Mama. Drew and I are going to get married. I'm looking into married housing tomorrow. It'll be exactly like you and Daddy when you were young."

Mama turned and stared at me for a moment, her eyes bleak and weary. She reached out to take my hand, but stopped as our fingers touched, leaving me aching. She opened her mouth to speak, raked her hand through her blond hair before realizing they were still covered in dirt, then whirled around and stomped into the house. The red door slammed and the windows shook behind her.

Chapter Three

Purdy

I hung my rusty old body over the ceramic pedestal tub, arms deep in bleach water, trying to clean the world's most stubborn tub ring once again. Disgusting. I couldn't stand the look of it, even though no one else ever came into this bathroom or used the tub. It haunted me, taunting me with its refusal to do what I wanted. I pulled a pad of steel wool out of the cleaning bucket and began scrubbing as a memory flashed through my mind.

I was seven years old the first time I realized how sick my mother was. The first time she tried to kill me. It was early summer. Freedom from school hung foremost in my mind and I planned my days long and wide, allowing plenty of time away from the house. The salamanders were out in full force, and easy to catch—though I'd been warned nearly on the hour by Mother not to touch them lest I get leprosy, or lose all my teeth. Looking back now, I can't believe I ever sought out those nasty things.

But that June morning, the air was warm and moist, the perfect time for trapping. The sweet smell of honeysuckle filled the air. I stopped along the way to pluck a few flowers and suck out the honey as Daddy taught me. Mother had taken to sleeping in late, and Granny Finn, her mother, had taken to raising Charlotte for the most part. I don't recall where Granny Finn was that day, but I can tell you for certain I knew every step she took from that day forward. I soon clung to her like my own life.

I'd snuck down to the creek behind our property being careful to follow the worn trail and avoid the corn fields, which Mother said were full of rattlesnakes. Six salamanders swam in a bucket by the time I heard her calling for me. Her voice was tense and frantic and I knew my day was over. Though I hated to do it, I tossed those slimy little suckers back into the creek and rushed down the trail toward home. I tried my best to check the sundress I'd chosen that morning—a sienna color—hoping she wouldn't notice any spots of red clay I'd happened to miss. But, I didn't take into account the speckled splashes of red that clung to the back of my legs. If it weren't for that, I'd have been home free.

From the second my eyes met Mother's, I knew I was in for it. Usually she'd yell a lot and force me to take another bath while she lectured me on cleanliness being after godliness, or some such nonsense. I could tell this time was different, but I didn't care. I was sick to death of her crazy ways. Always twitching and embarrassing me and Daddy. I was glad Charlotte was still a baby and I could tell her how things really should be—instead of the way things were around here.

Pacing, Mother continued with her usual ranting, while I pretended like I was somewhere else. Someone else. I only remember doing as I was told, as Granny Finn warned me to do so many times.

"Get into the bathroom, this instant."

"Yes, ma'am."

"Take off those nasty clothes and draw yourself a bath."

"Yes, ma'am."

"Wash that disease-infested slime off, before I come and do it for you."

"Yes, ma'am."

Mother was not one to put up with messes of any kind. And she was becoming more and more fanatical about cleanliness. Telling me always that it was how God wanted things. She never let a housekeeper near our home, even though every neighbor in the area had one. She insisted on cleaning everything herself. Sterilizing it thoroughly, as she put it. I'd watched her wash her hands so many times one evening after dinner that her knuckles bled from the incessant scrubbing. Later she'd stood at the sink flirting with Daddy as he held her hands under the cool water and let it run over the lacerations. She prattled on about his job, the neighborhood, the upcoming Parker family reunion, and such silly things, as if it was a normal way to spend time with your husband.

* * *

That summer morning, I sank into the lukewarm water and slid beneath, drowning out her voice as she stomped up and down the hall gathering her cleaning items. The silence felt good. Peaceful. I could imagine heaven and God and all the things she told me I'd have one day if I'd straighten up and behave.

I held my breath as long as I could, letting my face rise to the top only enough that I could let my mouth form a little "o", take another breath, and sink back under. With my eyes closed, I counted how long I could stay under. Well, most of me anyway.

Seventy-five seconds. One hundred seconds. A little "o" rising. One hundred and thirty. One hundred and forty-five. A little "o".

At two hundred, I opened my eyes under the water and could see a blurred moving version of Mother standing over me and turning her hand to the side. My little "o" quickly sputtered at whatever she was pouring on top of me. It burned, and I was choking, trying to get it out of me. Within seconds, I'd thrown up all over myself.

I rose to stand, buck-naked in the tub and crying. Mother held a bottle of straight bleach and a Brillo pad in her hand.

"Mother, what are you—"

She grabbed my arm and began to scrub. Rubbing hard, making me wince and pull from her. "Ow. Stop it!" My throat burned. "I need some water. Mother, please! I don't feel good."

"You hush, you hear me? I've got to get that off of you. Out of you. I don't want to catch—drink this."

She handed me a glass, as if full of water, goading me with a sweet smile.

I lifted it to my mouth, the smell of bleach rising and burning my nostrils.

"I can't drink that. It's poison, see? It'll make me sick again." I pointed to the skull and crossbones sign on the back. The same one they'd shown us in school and told us never to touch. Now, my own mother was trying to kill me with it.

"Never mind that. Do as you're told, Darlin'." Mother pushed my hand toward my mouth again this time using her sweet voice.

"No!" Everything in me wanted to get out of that tub.

"Drink it. This instant!" She screamed at me shaking her head from side to side.

"I can't. My teacher said—"

Before I could get the words out, the glass dropped into the tub, clinking to the bottom as Mother's hand wacked me across my face and threw me off balance. I started crying, partly from the slap, and partly from the fact I thought the bleach was going to eat me alive in that tub.

Mother peered at me with wide eyes. Then, as if turned by a switch, her countenance changed completely. Pulling me out of the tub, she covered my shoulders with a scratchy white towel, and sat me down on the makeup stool I was told never to sit on.

She lowered to her knees and stared me right in the eyes, brushing my tears away with the sleeve of her gauzy nightgown.

"Now, now, Darlin'. Hush, now. It's ok. You're clean now. Just perfect."

I sat stunned on the stool as she took the time to towel dry my hair and brush out the tangles, as gentle as she'd ever done it. Watching her from the mirror, her blue eyes darted as she took care of me. I wondered how someone could be so crazy and so sweet at the same time. I asked God to take the crazy out of me right then and there. But I was beginning to understand it was too late for Mother.

The memory fell as my cell phone buzzed on the counter. I cleared my throat, pushing the lump out of the way. Charlotte was calling. Again. Some nerve after skipping out on our lunch.

"Hello?" I put on my sweet voice. It always annoyed Charlotte.

"Can we talk, Purdy? It's about Janie."

"Who is this?"

"It's Charlotte. You know it's me. Plus, it's right there on your phone screen. Can I come over or not?"

"Oh. Well, hey there, Charlotte. Of course you can come over, Darlin'. There isn't a problem is there?" Of course I knew the problem. Any idiot could see it coming. Plus, I had my ways.

"I'll tell you about it when I get there," Charlotte said and hung up the phone.

I slapped the phone onto the counter and was startled by Tizzy, my precious tabby, as she jumped at the noise. "You know, it's a miracle she can even pick out her own underwear, Tizzy. I'm forced to take care of everything in this family." Tizzy wound around my ankles, leaning in to love on me. I patted her head, repositioning the bow on her collar the groomer tied the day before. If only everyone were a cat.

I pulled off my cleaning gloves and washed my hands at the sink. Wisps of graying blond hair waved at me as I stared into the mirror. Charlotte kept insinuating I dye it, but what did she know? Gray was a sign of grace and wisdom as far as I was concerned. Plus, I liked to remind her that she's the one who gave me all this gray—a comment she still despised from my first gray strand until today. So, of course, I had to keep it. Still, the disorder would never do. I took care to replace each piece, put on my rose lipstick, and smacked at my reflection. Perfect.

Removing my cleaning apron, I brushed off my capris, thankful I'd ironed them earlier. I watched my reflection once more, breathing in deeply. Once. Twice. Three times. I'd figure out something to take care of this. As a matter of fact, an idea was already brewing.

Chapter Four

Charlotte

Placing the phone on the counter, I realized it and my hands were still covered in potting soil. I lingered at the kitchen sink as I rinsed and watched Janie crying on the backyard swing. My heart ached for her, but I couldn't simply make this okay. On the one hand, I wanted to. I did. But, on the other . . . I mean, what about the rest of us? This was a small town. Too small. What about what it could mean for me?

Flashes of her as a young child filled my mind. Janie wearing a sundress covered in dirt from pulling flowers out of my garden to give to me. Janie soaking wet holding a snapping turtle and crying because she didn't know how to put it down without getting bitten. The two of us, tanned and smelling of coconut sunscreen, eating popsicles on the back patio. How had we gotten to this point so fast?

Surely Purdy already knew. She couldn't—or wouldn't—hide her excitement over the phone. I could tell she was enjoying it.

Worse than that, I wouldn't be allowed to handle this my way. The Parkers had a hierarchy, and I was clearly at the bottom.

A lifetime surrounded by Parker women—more than anything else—taught me what was expected from me as I watched them dissect each and every woman who crossed their path. They noted people's failures with a tinge of happiness that made me cringe. They teased me ruthlessly for my "tenderheartedness" and considered me weak because of it. I wasn't like them and often wondered if it was because I was raised by my Daddy, or because I wasn't raised by Mama.

Growing up, my cousins, Purdy and I spent our Saturday's working the counter in my daddy's clothing store. I watched helplessly each week as some poor thing would wander in looking for a pair of underwear and before she'd even laid them on the counter to purchase, the Parker women decided what kind of man she would marry and which trailer park they would live in. They showed mercy to no one, including me.

I'd heard the things people thought about Mama. It didn't mean I took them to heart. Small towns could be a relentless breeding ground of gossip. Ones that forced the sins of your family on you no matter what you did to escape them or prove yourself otherwise. As much as I liked to think of Mama exactly like me, most people acted as if that should be the last thing I desired. I tucked what tiny memories I had of her in the sweet spots of my mind, savoring the good. Purdy encouraged the same, and in many ways, she'd been the only Mama I'd ever really known.

I discovered what was required of me early in life, but struggled not to deviate. Purdy did everything she could to train me in her ways, but they just never took. I never seemed to live up to the high expectations of anyone in my family; so I quit trying. I found solace in the place many young girls do—a young man. What began as the most wonderful thing to ever happen to me, David, ended with me pregnant and us being forced to marry. I put my dreams to the side, saving them for my daughter.

Now I wondered if not telling her about my own mistakes, had been a mistake. Maybe my life could have sounded as a warning. But, it was too late for warnings now.

I checked myself in the hall mirror, choking back my emotions once more. I didn't want to unravel in front of Purdy, but I knew I probably would, and Purdy would enjoy watching it firsthand. Like a spider relishing a fly as it crawled onto her web.

I left by the front entrance, hoping Janie wouldn't notice I was gone, or what direction I'd headed. My steps were heavy along the brick side walk that wound through the lawn down toward the street. Monkey grass dotted the central flower bed, though I was sure I'd told the landscaper not to use it this year. What else had I failed to notice?

My breathing quickened as I stepped onto the paved walk that trailed through the neighborhood, gearing up for the confrontation. I didn't want Janie to be pressured to marry as I had been, even though life for David and I turned out better than I ever expected. We'd been lucky to discover how perfectly matched we were. In fact, considering how much I clung to him in the beginning—how I gasped for his attention like air—our relationship was incredibly grounded...

Still, I ached over losing my dreams. I'd always hoped to break away from the Parkers. To do something that was mine alone. But apparently, that ache would continue for a lifetime. Janie's pregnancy was just another nail, holding me in my place.

As I walked, I glanced at the stately old homes that stood in a neat row on each side of the street. Each boasted acre lawns that rolled down to the sidewalk. Nearly every home in the neighborhood was on the historic registry with luscious gardens in the back and wide-plank porches wrapping around the perimeter. They seemed so pristine, so perfect. Million dollar sink holes, David called them.

In the early years of our marriage, we'd spent months renovating and revitalizing our home to its former glory. We had the one house on the block proven to have been slept in by

Robert E. Lee. But, things of that nature were really wasted on me. As much as my family wanted me to, I couldn't care less about social boosters—a fact Purdy especially despised.

Three doors down, Purdy perched on her rocking chair, seeming to enjoy the image of me rushing to her for advice. A tray of cookies and sweet tea sat between her and where she motioned me to sit. I slid into the rocker, marveling at the perfect row of them aligning both sides of the front door. I'd never seen Purdy use them and it occurred to me she'd probably never had enough people visit at one time to fill all the spots. Another show, it would seem.

"You knew, didn't you?" I pressed, my face warming.

"Well, of course I knew. Good gravy, Charlotte, any fool could see it."

"But, she's barely pregnant. She's not even showing yet. How could you possibly—"

"Pregnant?" Purdy's eyes widened.

I panicked. Was there something else?

"You mean to tell me, my niece is preggers? At the age of twenty? What? Did you tell her your story like a fairy tale all these years, so she wanted to follow in your embarrassing footsteps? Good gracious, Charlotte. This is ridiculous."

"Well, what else did you think it was? You were dropping hints left and right, lording some big secret over me. I thought you knew."

"Of course I didn't know. After all these years you'd think you'd wise up. Can't you tell a bluff when you see one, you ninny?"

My jaw tightened, my fists pulling into balls. Why couldn't I stand up to her? "Why would you do that to me, Purdy? We're grown women! This is your family too, whether you like it or not. Janie's your niece."

"Well, she may be my niece, but it won't be me everyone lays the blame on. Of course, we'll take care of it before it comes to that. We can't allow this to happen every two decades in the

Parker line. The whole town will pitch a fit. You know what we must do, Charlotte."

"No. I'm not going to force her to marry Drew. She's halfway through college. She needs to finish."

"Well, of course not. She's not marrying that white trash. There's only one option."

"No, Purdy."

"Well, what then? It's not going to disappear on its own. Grow up for once."

My breath caught. What options did we have? This would kill my Daddy, and he was sick enough. Regardless of what Janie wanted to do, we wouldn't be given a choice. Purdy would stop at nothing to make this disappear. I sat in silence, scrambling for an idea.

"Oh, fine! I'll take care of it, as always," Purdy flew out of her chair, to stand in front of me.

"Take care of it how—"

"Listen, if you're not going to take charge here, I will. I'll figure it out and fill you in on the plan." Purdy's head shook slightly, as she pinched the bridge of her nose.

"You're not in charge here, Purdy. She's my daughter." My throat tightened.

"And a fine one at that, we all see."

"Worse things happen. We can think of something else." I straightened up in the chair.

Purdy grabbed my elbow and pulled me closer, her grip tightening with every hateful word. "I'm taking care of this whether you like it or not. It's a Parker battle now. You do as you're told, Charlotte, or you'll regret it."

A strange combination of power and fear seemed to fill her steel blue eyes. For the first time in my life, I considered she might really be crazy. Certifiable. I wished I'd stayed home and dealt with Janie myself. A traitor—that was all I would become to my daughter now. The rest of them would see me for the coward they'd always suspected.

Purdy dropped my wrist and closed her eyes, shaking her head as if to reset her mind. When she opened them, a sweet smile spread across her face and she leaned over me to retrieve the plates and glasses.

"Now, shoo, butterfly," Purdy mocked. It was the nickname she'd given me as a child. More for being an overweight annoyance than a thing of beauty.

I stepped uneasily down the porch and was half way down the sidewalk before looking back. The rocking chairs slowed, slipping back to their immaculate positions, as if a convincing accomplice in a cover-up.

* * *

Pausing at my own front steps, I watched David's car pull into the garage and dreaded what was coming. I hoped his day at the store had been a good one. Hurrying into the kitchen, I found Janie sitting on a barstool at the island, texting. We glanced at each other without speaking. My heart ached, but my anger built.

The dinner I'd prepped earlier made me sick to think about. I began pulling items from the fridge and suddenly remembered the chicken I'd left baking in the oven. Yanking it from the rack, I hoped it wasn't dry. Again.

David came in from the garage and poked his head around the kitchen door, hanging up his car keys. His tie hung crooked, like a noose. The grey hair that fringed his sideburns seemed to be spreading, yet it took nothing away from his charm.

"How're my girls?" He sounded so upbeat, so blind.

Don't ask.

David slid beside Janie on another barstool as she began chopping up vegetables for the salad. Popping a sliver of carrot into his mouth, he patted Janie on the back and kissed her forehead, his evening routine.

"Good day, Janie?"

"Um-hmm."

Without thinking, my head snapped in their direction. At least she avoided lying with actual words. A trick I wondered how frequently Janie used.

David caught my eye. "Everything okay, Char?"

I nodded and shooed him away with a wave of my hand. "Dinner will be ready in a moment, David. Why don't you go into the living room while Janie and I finish getting everything ready?"

His mouth pulled downward as if confused, but obliged anyway. I watched as he went to sit in his leather chair, grabbed the remote lying beside it, and flipped on ESPN.

After placing the biscuits in the oven, I heated up the frying pan. As the oil warmed, I crept to the edge of the living room. Watching David sitting in his chair, knowing what was to come over dinner, was painful. I glanced around the room, my gaze resting on the family portrait above the stone fireplace and wished I wasn't about to ruin everything.

This was the one place in my life I felt safe from the constant turmoil. Yet, it managed to creep in. The ladies at the club would torment me next Monday. And, the rest of the Parkers—well— they'd been expecting something like this for twenty years.

Janie continued to putter around the kitchen, stopping to text while putting out plates, placing napkins, and gathering silverware. I couldn't bear to look at her, and knew I wouldn't be able to contain myself over dinner. For the first time in my life, I felt hate toward my daughter, a truth that both scared and shamed me.

Janie's phone buzzed and she punched at it again, a motion that highly irritated me. I would never understand the constant need to feel connected like that. I liked to be away. Freedom from others seemed a frivolous pleasure, not a hole to be filled.

I turned my back to Janie and filled the plates with baked chicken, fried okra, and mashed potatoes. Janie placed the salad in the center of the table and filled glasses with ice, ready for the sweet tea. I checked the baking powder biscuits in the oven one last time, feeling Janie's eyes on me as I made my way through the kitchen. I didn't speak to her—or even look in her direction. I wanted to push myself far away from this life ahead of us. Away from what she'd done to me.

"Dinner." My voice felt dry, unlike my usual, perky invitation.

David took his seat as Janie and I took ours, facing each other.

"So, who can tell me something good today?" David always started dinner this way.

I directed my glare at Janie. All at once I was overwhelmed. Hate, loss, and regret sunk deep into my heart, and I wanted her to feel it too. The powerless position. The utter lack of control. All of it was hers, not mine. Hers.

"Well, Janie has some news, if that's what you mean." My voice was flat, my eyes boring into Janie's as I continued to chew my food. "Go ahead, tell him."

"Mama, no—"

"Oh? No? So you do know the word." I focused my eyes on my plate, hating to hear my own voice. My jaw tightened, and I set my fork down for the battle.

"Charlotte, what's wrong with you two?" David gave a nervous smile, looking back and forth between us. "We only get Janie for a couple of weeks before she has to go back for exams. Whatever it is can't be that bad. I had a nice weekend planned for us. Dinner at Marchiano's tomorrow night. Won't that be—"

"She's pregnant," I blurted then pushed away from the table. "Pregnant, David!" I threw my napkin down, a desperation filling me that I despised. Both of them stared at me, as if they didn't get it. Why were they so calm? Couldn't they see what this meant? For them? For me? A guttural scream exploded from my lungs. I picked up the salad bowl and threw it across the room. Red and yellow shards of porcelain mingled with salad oil, oozing along the grout channels of the terracotta tiled floor.

Janie looked terrified and I immediately regretted what I'd done. She stared at me, blinking hard, and then hung her head. My hand flew to my mouth, cupping the gasps that tried to escape. My vision darted from Janie, to David, to the mess on the floor. I stepped carefully behind David, stopping a moment to touch his shoulder in some meager attempt to place us on the same side.

"Mama, I'm so sorry," Janie whispered.

"No. It's me. I am." My heart broke. I pressed toward Janie, grief stricken, and touched her hair as I passed to clean up the mess I'd made.

David stood up and pushed his chair away from the table.

"I'm so sorry, Daddy. Let me explain. Please," Janie pleaded as she watched her father follow in my path. Janie squeezed her eyes shut and laid her head in her hands.

I closed my eyes as well, not wanting to watch anymore. Disowned. That's what the Parker's would insist for Janie if she didn't marry immediately. Or take care of it otherwise. Our family had rules. The kind which were never forgotten. I was all too familiar with them.

David came beside me and took my elbow. I held the broken shards dripping with oil. My shoulders shook as a sob rose up in my throat that I couldn't contain. The sound of my cries filled the room. Still holding me, he turned to Janie and moved us both behind her, clasping her shoulder, linking us together.

Janie's body jerked at the touch, and he dropped my elbow to tend to her. As he slid his arms around her, Janie's entire body sank into him as she wept. My hand hung loose, alone again.

"I love you, Janie," he whispered, pulling her close and rubbing her back. Always her comforter, even as she ruined his family.

The sight of it all was too much. I left the room, defeated. The slamming of my bedroom door echoed through the house.

Chapter Five

Janie

My fingers moved frantically as I texted Drew. Where was he? I needed to get a better handle on what happened. I couldn't believe they found out before I had a chance to tell them. How could I be so careless?

My phone buzzed

SORRY BABE. I'M HOME.

My fingers struggled to type, and I switched to calling instead. I'd already talked to the campus housing department earlier and knew I'd feel so much better if I could get all that worked out with Drew.

"Hey, I um . . . meant to call you last night," Drew whispered. "I got stuck at this party with my old high school buddies. I had to sneak in at like, three in the morning. You having fun being home?"

"Um. I don't know if I'd call it that. Mama found out."

"I knew you shouldn't have told them yet, Janie. We needed a plan first. What if things change now? If we decide to do something else, they'll totally know."

"Something else? We already have a plan, Drew. Remember? I even called the housing department today and put us on a list for one of the remaining apartments. There are three left, but we need to get them a deposit by next week or our name falls off the list. You can do that, right? I'm completely broke."

"Um . . . yeah. I guess I can ask my mom. But, she's going to freak."

"Well, you have to tell her anyway, right? At least this way she'll know we've made a plan, like we have it all under control and stuff."

"Yeah . . ." Drew's voice faded and I could hear some muffled talking in the background.

"Who's that?"

"Oh. Um. My mom just walked in. I need to go."

"You're going to tell her, right?"

"Yeah . . ." Drew let out a long breath. It sounded like he was holding his hand over the receiver as he whispered something to someone beside him. I felt shoved to the side.

"Is someone else there?"

"What? No. It's just . . . um, my mom. I've got to go."

Not convincing. "Okay. Well, I'll call you back later. I'm pretty sure Mama's monitoring my every move right now. So, I'll wait until she goes to bed. I love you."

"You too," Drew whispered into the phone and then hung up.

I stood in the center of the room, talking myself out of the doubt that now plagued my thoughts. I pulled out my laptop, clicked on the Google bar, and typed "baby names". That would get me focused back in the right direction. As I browsed, I imagined what my little boy or girl might look like.

In my mind, each had dark hair like mine and green eyes like Drew. Ringlet curls—even though we both had stick straight hair—and perfect rose colored lips. I imagined them in Christmas card pictures hanging ornaments on the tree, smiling at me from my old tree house, and running through the sprinklers at the Parker homestead. The last image seemed tainted somehow. The Parkers would never let that happen. I knew exactly what this pregnancy would mean to them. I would be punished, not celebrated. By the time I crawled into my bed, it was well after midnight. The moon rose above the old magnolia and peeked through the wide leaves, hidden from being fully seen.

I hadn't seen or spoken to Mama and Daddy since dinner, and it was too late to call Drew back now. I searched one more site, determined to find the perfect name. Who knew there were so many? Or that they actually had different meanings? That, of course, made it even harder. I mean, I was blessing or cursing them for life, right? But, before I pushed the laptop to the side and closed my eyes, I'd settled on two: Eva and Eli. Hoping I wouldn't need both.

I pulled up the patchwork quilt Grandma Johnston had given me as a young girl, and drew it in all around me. As I looked up at the ceiling, I had the sudden urge to do something I hadn't done in a long time.

God, help me be a good Mama. In spite of myself.

* * *

The phone buzzing on my nightstand woke me up. Groggy, I patted around for the device, pushing books to the floor and almost spilling a glass of stale water that had likely been there for days. I tapped the side key, and tried to focus...

CAN I COME C U TODAY?

It was Drew. Relief flowed through my body. I knew he'd come around. I texted my reply, and rolled out of bed, headed for the shower. In the sudden rush, my stomach lurched and I hurried to the toilet instead. I knew this was just the beginning of such things.

I rinsed my mouth in the sink, and stood to watch myself in the mirror. My skin seemed almost dewy, despite how I felt inside. I checked the clock on my cell and realized it was Saturday. Being away from campus had really thrown my sense of time off. I was supposed to go shopping with Mama today. I quickly texted Drew back that he would have to wait, and asked him to call me later instead.

I struggled in the shower, trying to keep my mind and my stomach steady. I toweled off and dressed in a spaghetti strapped sundress, then pulled my wet hair into a loose bun. Walking downstairs to wait in the kitchen, I hoped today would be better. Mama never carried a grudge. Said it was how God wanted us to be. Surely, we could at least talk about it. The day I'd been looking forward to for weeks suddenly seemed like a thing to be dreaded.

I waited for a good twenty minutes before I decided to go check on her. Mama was late getting up, which was unusual for someone who spent most Saturdays in the garden starting at daybreak. I finally had to go and knock on her door.

"Mama? Are we still going shopping?"

I pushed the door slightly to find Mama and Daddy's bed made and no sign of them anywhere. I checked the counter in the kitchen—not even a note. Mama had left without me.

I sank onto the kitchen stool again, completely depressed. My head pounded and I pressed my temples in an attempt to relieve the pressure. The scent of bananas from the fruit bowl filled my senses and I considered making Mama some banana bread—her favorite—as an apology. I'd hoped we would have another chance to talk things through. I mean, if I could get her to talk to me, she would understand, right? My hands fell to my lap and I realized there was no sense in wearing a dress if I didn't have to. I wandered into the laundry room, searching for a pair of old jeans and a tee shirt, then slipped into the powder room and changed.

From the foyer, I heard the front door click as if someone was sneaking in—or out. I hurried through the house and rushed to the window. Tiptoeing across the porch and out onto the lawn, was Mama. She slinked toward Purdy's Lexus, as if she needed to hide from me, dressed in one of her Saturday frocks.

I have to tell you, that lit me on fire. I mean, she was sneaking away from me? She was choosing Purdy over me? I grabbed my purse and headed to my own car in the garage, slamming the door behind me.

In town, I drifted up and down the streets, passing the little boutiques on Main we always shopped on the weekends. I don't know what I was thinking I'd do. Jump out and say "got-cha!" if I saw Mama and Purdy shopping together? Most of the stores were in morning prep mode, sweeping the sidewalk and watering the blossoming flowers at the curb. I felt drawn to pull my car onto a side street and find an inconspicuous parking spot, like I was undercover or something. I thought of Mama and wished things weren't so bad between us. I missed her even if I was mad as a hornet.

Glancing in my mirror, my eyes seemed swollen and sunken all at once. I pushed through fast food bags and loose leaf papers in the back floorboards to find a black sweater Jenn left there months before. I wasn't exactly a cleaner.

Zipping up the sweater seemed ridiculous in such heat, but it hid my ratty tee shirt and maybe the fact that despite my best efforts, my belly was beginning to expand. At least it seemed bigger to me. I tucked the strings from my jeans underneath the hem and got out of the car. Keeping an eye on everyone who passed, but trying not to be seen, I shuffled slowly along as if window shopping.

Baby B's, a store I'd never noticed before, suddenly stuck out to me. I stood at the window, eyeing the fuzzy polka-dotted blankets, tiny patent leather shoes, and monogrammed pacifiers.

I pushed the door open, clicking a switch that caused a robot-like lullaby to play over the doorbell system. A woman pushing a designer pram scrutinized me up and down as she stood at one of the racks. Her eyes lingered on my stomach. My gaze felt forced downward, and I wished I'd thought before coming inside.

From the back room, a petite brunette in a ruffled maternity blouse and high heels waddled her way over to me, carrying a basket full of stacked baby blankets. "All blankets are thirty percent off today. Let me know if you need any help, hon."

I smiled and nodded. "Okay, thanks. I'm just, um . . . looking." Looking for what?

Brightly colored textures surfaced everything I touched as I circled the racks. I'd never seen such tiny mittens or socks. I'd never heard of "pee-pee tee-pees." Who knew babies needed such things?

I felt pulled to the frilly side of the store and quietly made my way through a stack of pink and orange smocked dresses stacked neatly on a shelf. Matching socks designed to look like tiny shoes dotted the frame, and I could hardly contain a laugh building inside. Baskets full of miniature hats and sunglasses sat atop each clothing rack. Sunglasses?

"Looking for anything in particular?" The saleslady slid beside me and pulled out a yellow knit jumper. "We just got this in. It would be perfect for a boy or a girl, if you aren't going to find out, that is."

Could she tell? I looked up at her suddenly, then down again. I fingered the jumper and held it up in front of me, to be polite, of course. "I like pink."

"A girl? Oh, honey, you'll love a girl. So many bows, so many shoes. They are fun, fun, fun to shop for! When are you due?"

Due? The thought hadn't occurred to me. Dr. Franklin, my childhood pediatrician, crossed my thoughts. What would he think of me now? Disappointment followed everyone I touched.

"Um. I don't know yet," I mumbled. Tears filled my eyes and I moved toward another rack, trying to avoid conversation.

"Oh. I'm sorry to be so nosey. Ignore me, honey. I just love babies. I get so excited for everyone that comes in here. I can't help myself. I'm sorry, really."

The first kindness shown to me since the news came out was more than I could handle. My throat ached as I strained to hold back. My body began shaking and a gasp escaped.

"Oh honey—don't. Don't cry. You're going to be fine."

"You don't understand . . . I'm still in school. My parents hate me now—well, not my dad . . . but my mom, she definitely hates me."

"Oh, Darlin', I'm sure they don't hate you. Parents can't actually hate their kids, it's genetically impossible. They might be upset—or surprised—but they don't hate you."

"You don't know my mom." I walked back toward the front door, wondering if anyone might see me coming out. Great Janie, show the whole world, why don't you? The woman with the pram stood to the side texting with a smirk on her face. Was she making fun of me to her haughty friends? I wanted to crawl under something and hide.

"You know, I had my first baby when I was young too." The saleslady came from behind me and held out the tiniest pair of pink booties I'd ever seen. "God will take care of you, sweetie. You and that precious little baby. This is a gift." She held the booties toward me and for a moment I wasn't sure if she meant them, or the baby.

A huff of breath came from the corner of the store, and I caught pram-Mama eyeing me with disdain. I cupped the booties in the palm of my hand. So small, they didn't even stretch to my fingers. Pink knitted stitches circled around, topped with white lace. A pink ribbon wove through the edges and spilled over the top, tied in a bow. I wondered if my baby had toes yet.

I opened my mouth to speak, but couldn't find the words.

"You don't need to thank me, honey. Remember, it's a gift."

I walked closer to the door, nodding on auto-pilot and grabbed the door handle as the robot-melody sounded again.

"Oh! One more thing." The saleslady ran to the checkout area and fumbled around for a few seconds before rushing back over. She held a booklet between both hands, as if praying over it, and then handed it to me. "I want you to keep this too. It's something that helped me get through my first. I'm so grateful I had her, though I didn't realize it at the time. And please, come back and see me again. Bring that baby girl with you, you hear?"

I took the book. Choosing Motherhood curled in white letters across the top. A picture of a white baby blanket with tiny toes peeking out lay beneath the title. I couldn't contain my smile any longer. The toes would be my favorite part.

I tucked the book under my arm, and glanced along the street as I stepped out of the store and into the Saturday morning foot traffic on Main. A lanky teenager talking on her cell phone while walking beside her mother nearly ran into me. Gathering Jenn's sweater around me, I shivered as goose bumps pricked my arms. I held the booties in my hand, concealing my secret gift.

Chapter Six

Purdy

I sat with Charlotte at her ratty old kitchen table, the brochures fanned in front of us. Why she didn't talk David into getting her some decent furniture in here was beyond me. Janie was apparently out gallivanting around doing God knows what, and I hoped David would keep himself busy at the store—lest I have to get ugly.

But, before we even got good and started, Charlotte nearly jumped out of her skin as the back screen door pushed open, and Janie stepped into the kitchen. She gathered up the papers in one quick motion, then held them on her lap. The whole thing was ridiculous, if you asked me. I mean, who was running this train wreck, anyway?

"Running out and about again, Janie? Really. Are you a total derelict?" I stifled a laugh as anger flashed in Janie's eyes. Like she had any right to be angry at us.

Charlotte kicked me under the table, and I nearly snapped my heel off trying to stomp her big toe in response. Charlotte watched Janie and then turned to me with a pitiful look in her eye. Pleading. I could tell she wanted to get up and hug Janie. Make it all better, and what-not. If it weren't for the brochures hiding, it would've been a regular love fest in there.

"I needed to think," Janie pushed out through clenched teeth. She shuffled past us and stopped at the foot of the back stairs. "And, I thought we were going shopping this morning, Mama. I guess I got my day wrong. So, I went by myself."

"Well, we're fully aware of what a planner you are lately. Thought a lot about this little predicament, didn't you?" I said. It felt so good getting that out.

Janie glared at me, her face reddening, then glanced at Charlotte. Like she could help. Apparently not finding what she was looking for, Janie clenched her teeth once more and returned on her path up the stairs.

I could hear her crying as she turned the corner on the landing and continued to her room.

For a split second, I felt for her. I mean, I'm not totally heartless. An image came back to me of climbing the stairs and crying as Mother mumbled hateful things about me in the kitchen below. I knew what it was to be a disappointment. That's why we had to take care of this. She could move on freely after this. Forgiven.

"Tell her now, Charlotte—before she gets any other grand ideas."

"I know. I just really feel like I should talk to David first. What if he doesn't think we—"

"Good gravy, Charlotte. Are you really going to let her ruin her entire life over this? I've listened to you lament about all the things you missed out on, for twenty years. David would agree. Go get her. Now. We're doing this."

Like a reprimanded child, Charlotte took the steps. Some things were just too easy.

Chapter Seven

Charlotte

Easing down the hall, I was surprised to find Janie's door open and her sitting on her bed as if waiting for me. I sat beside her and put my arm around her trying to make amends. Guilt flooded over me as she leaned into my embrace.

"We need you to come down and talk about all this, Janie."

"I don't want to talk with Aunt Purdy here, Mama. She makes everything worse. I hate talking to her."

Janie chewed on a nail and I had to fight the urge to push her hand away. She wasn't a child anymore.

"She has to be tough, Janie. She's what holds this family together. It's what she's good at, I suppose."

"She holds this family hostage, is more like it."

I sputtered a laugh, surprising myself.

Janie laughed a little too, and leaned into me, increasing my guilt.

"Why don't you take a shower and get yourself dressed. Then, you can come down when you're ready. I'll keep her at bay until then."

"I've already showered, Mama. And, I am dressed."

"Oh. Right." I didn't want to argue about her clothes again. "Okay, then. Just come on when you're ready, okay?"

Janie nodded and lay back on her bed raking her hand through her hair.

I retreated to the kitchen to find Purdy on her cell, looking out the window toward my garden. It struck me that there might be something out there that would clue her into my plan to leave the family business. If there was, I hoped she was too preoccupied to notice.

"Yes. The second light. Got it." Purdy turned to me, her eyes closed, as if imagining the route.

A board creaked as I stepped in the room and Purdy's eyes opened, an immediate look of disgust flashing across her face. She snapped her old phone shut.

"Where's Janie? Do I have to do everything around here?" She clipped toward the steps.

I put my hand out to block her. "She's coming. Give her a moment."

Purdy couldn't contain herself. She was by far, the most impatient person I'd ever met. She hated to be kept waiting and eventually went into the back yard, where I figured she'd sneak a cigarette. I'd discovered her butt-burial-spot years before, but never mentioned it. Somehow knowing it was there made her self-righteousness easier for me to bear.

Thankfully, Janie came down while Purdy was occupied. I walked to her and hugged her, rubbing her back.

"It's going to be okay, Janie. I know I've not handled this well. It's just . . .well. We only want what's best for you. And your future. I know this all seems black and white to you, but having a family at a young age is very difficult. You have no idea."

"I know, Mama. That's why I wanted to talk to you about it. You and Daddy seemed to handle it so well. Drew and I admire that about the two of you. We want to do as good a job for our baby, as you did for me. I've known about all that for years."

The comment pierced me and I inadvertently sucked in a breath.

"What?" Had my situation somehow given her permission?

Purdy bounded up the back steps, letting the back screen door slam as she came into the kitchen. She took David's seat at the head of the table and motioned for Janie and me to sit. We took our common spots, facing each other. Neither of us would look in Purdy's direction.

"I'm really sorry you feel like I've let you down, Aunt Purdy," Janie started. "But, you're making too big a deal about all of this. Really. Drew and I are getting married. We've talked about all of it. I've reserved an apartment for us in married housing. We even discussed running down to Dillon and getting married in one of those little roadside chapels. It'll be cute. Really. I don't need more than that."

I heard the young hope in Janie's voice and wanted to agree. But, as I turned to gauge Purdy's reaction, a sour scowl of disapproval engraved her features.

"Married, Janie? That's ridiculous," Purdy practically spat the words. "And, how exactly do you plan to raise a baby in married housing? What about studying? Do you have any idea how much sleep you won't be getting after the baby gets here? You won't be able to concentrate for two minutes, much less study."

I reluctantly joined in, knowing Purdy was right. At least about that. "Drew's not even a grown man yet, Janie. You both need more control over your life. A baby complicates things in a way you can't even imagine. Like it was with—" I stopped.

Janie's eyes shot up to mine. Her eyes narrowed. "Like me? Was I . . . a complication?"

"No. I didn't mean it like that," I retreated.

"I think maybe you did, Mama. And, I think I'm getting a clearer picture of it all." Janie sat up straighter, and leaned forward, as if ready to take us on. She had no idea who she was dealing with.

"Janie . . . you were never a burden to me. It was just so—unexpected. And, then getting married so early. I sacrificed everything I wanted in life for—"

"Me. Yeah. I get it now. I don't know why I didn't figure this out earlier. This isn't even about me, is it? It's about me not becoming you."

My arms began itching terribly and I glanced down to discover I was breaking out in hives.

"Just so you know, I'm still planning on finishing college. Not that it's any of your business, Purdy. They won't kick me out because I'm pregnant."

"We won't let you do that, Janie—we won't allow it. You need to take care of this situation right away." Purdy straightened herself.

"What do you mean 'take care of it'? Why does everyone keep saying that? This isn't a problem to solve. It's a baby. It's your grandbaby, Mama." Janie's eyes softened as she reached for my hand, but I couldn't bear to offer it. I wouldn't support her throwing her life away.

"You're not thinking this through, Miss Priss," Purdy said. "You'll lose everything if you go through with this—your friends, your social life, and especially Drew." Purdy eased the look on her face, molding it into one of faux-kindness. Her ultimate manipulation tactic. She nudged me under the table.

"Just come with us to see the doctor, Janie," I pleaded. Surely he would talk some sense into her.

"Dr. Franklin?" Janie asked. She actually seemed interested in the idea. "Shouldn't I see a woman doctor or something?"

"Of course. No, not Dr. Franklin. We've found another doctor. Purdy already called and they are trying to work us in. You need to do this. Not only for yourself, Janie. For the entire family. Please," I urged hoping she'd accept. I knew Purdy would get her there one way or another. Plan B would not be pleasant.

"Okay, Mama. Fine. I was going to go see someone anyway. I'll go. Maybe they'll talk some sense into you. Things have changed a lot since you did this, you'll see."

I turned to Purdy, as worried as I've ever been. Purdy smiled a slow, satisfied smile. Victorious.

Chapter Eight

Janie

I willingly got into the Lexus with Purdy and Mama. I'd never seen Purdy so underdressed and frumpy looking. I didn't know she even owned such clothes. As usual, I climbed into the back seat behind her, positioning myself just so. I'd viewed half of my childhood from this vantage point, placing myself so I could see and talk to Mama while avoiding Purdy's gaze and sideward glances as much as possible. The looks Purdy gave me from the rear view mirror always gave me the willies.

We drove through town passing my life's landmarks. Market Park, where Daddy and I held private tea parties—sat right in the middle of town. I pictured him kneeling on the edge of a small pink blanket as I fed him crumbling peanut butter sandwiches and tiny cups of over-sugared lemonade. I remembered the cars driving by and honking as I served him. He'd never acted embarrassed or hurried me along, but instead would slump down and play along; wiping his mouth with the good linens I'd taken from the buffet drawer. I wished he was with us.

Turning onto Main Street, I leaned my head against the window toward Ginger's Spa and Salon, the central axis of the gossip and secrets of Riverton. It wasn't so much a spa as it was a hotbed of information. But, as times changed and Ginger felt the need to compete with the other hair salons popping up left and right in the mall, she hired Grady Culbert to carve a small "spa" sign that would sit at an angle on her current signage and save her the cost of a total overhaul. I could see the ladies through the front window as they sat in a circle of curlered heads, doing their best to keep everyone afloat on the comings and goings of local favorites, and especially the not-so-favorites. Mama and I'd spent hours in there each Saturday when I was younger, getting our hair and nails done. She was my best friend then.

Going further through town, we passed the road that led to Waymont High. Past the school I'd longed to be a part of as a preteen. Wishing my life away so I could be a cheerleader, I could drive a car, I could have a boyfriend. My thoughts settled on Drew. I'd always imagined him coming with me to pregnancy checkups. I thought of our baby and reached my hand into my purse to feel the small booties I'd received from the maternity store. I wished I'd talked more to the owner about how things had gone for her.

* * *

We continued past town to an area I'd never been through before. I faced the window and watched as well-groomed yards gave way to weeds at knee level. The smell of sulfur from the local paper mill forced itself through the air vents. I held my breath in, hoping it would soon pass.

The further from the city limits we drove, the more impoverished the area became. Trash dotted the street curb even as the sidewalks disappeared. Pedestrians in unkempt clothes gathered in groups of three or four and watched as we passed. I pulled my arms into my body wondering why on earth Mama would choose a doctor so out of the way.

"Why aren't we going to your doctor, Mama? He wouldn't tell anyone. I think it's against the law actually, for him to say anything."

"Read this," Purdy spit out a quick burst of air, making me feel small and insignificant as usual. She slid a brochure over the seat and let it drop at my feet.

I leaned over to pick it up and rose again to find Mama eyeing me through the makeup mirror as she supposedly touched up her nose. My head dizzied as I read statistics about abortion, the story of one woman who was successful in moving on in her life afterward, and medical details about what would happen in that kind of procedure.

"I am not getting an abortion." I was furious. "Where'd you get this, Purdy?"

Purdy adjusted the rear view mirror to better look at me and patted down her hair as if doing so might make her effort seem more credible. "I stopped in at the pregnancy center this morning. Thought you could use some information about your options, is all. You shouldn't throw your whole life away. My goodness, use your brain for once."

I didn't move a muscle, but they ached from the tension as I clinched my entire body at once. I tried to see Mama's face, but I could only glimpse her nose and mouth which seemed tense as if she were forbidden to speak. I knew she'd gone with Purdy.

"You don't believe in that kind of thing, do you, Mama?"

She sat silent.

"You've always said a child is a gift from God. That's how you explained Zee's situation to me when I was little. Only God can make or take a life. He has a plan for everyone. Isn't that what you said? "

No response.

"I've heard it a million times from you, Mama. Even when Zee gets on your last nerve, you always say it. Every child is a gift . . ."

Mama's mouth twitched and for a moment, I thought she would speak up. I thought she might save me from Purdy and her hideous plans. But she didn't. She stared straight ahead as if on some kind of mind altering drug. For the first time in my life, I hated my mother with everything I had.

"Exactly what kind of doctor are you taking me to?" my voice cracked. Panic was setting in and I wondered if jumping from a moving car on this side of town would garner pity from onlookers or pleasure in finding a wounded victim.

Purdy's knuckles turned white as she gripped the steering wheel full force. "Janie, it's best this way. You'll see."

I could not believe where I was and what they were asking me to do. "I'm not doing this, Purdy. I don't care what you say."

"Just go talk to him. That's all we're asking." Purdy tried to be inconspicuous as she pushed Mama. But Mama jumped in response, causing Purdy to exhale and roll her eyes.

"Just go talk to him, Janie." Mama said as the car pulled behind the building into the side parking lot of the Malton Family Planning Clinic.

Driving up to that place reminded me of standing before a summer storm just seconds before the rain comes. I could see it, like a slow evil you can't stop no matter how much you will it to. The moment darkness overtakes the landscape and tree lines fade to near black against a perfect blue sky. As the drops fall, everything is silenced and you are helpless. You must wait out a storm of that magnitude or be caught up in its destruction.

Chapter Nine

Purdy

Janie leaned her head against the window as I schlepped my carload of nincompoops into a large parking lot, then through a gated area to a smaller one. Fenced in on all sides, the small entrance allowed enough room for just one vehicle. A chunky man in white uniform, too small for his girth, stood by the gate gauging those who sought to enter. I imagined diseased rats hiding in every possible shadow.

I glanced at Janie, certain she was considering an escape. There was no chance of that. This wasn't my first barbeque, as they say. As we pulled into a spot, Janie jerked the handle of her door up, to no avail. She did it again, with no success.

Of course, I'd thought of that. When I was in control, I was in control. I gathered my things from the front seat and got out in my own time. I meandered over to Janie's side of the car and planted myself beside her door, watching her fume at me from the back seat. I opened the door and pointed to the metal switch on the inside of the doorframe. Child proof locks.

"You can't make me do this, Purdy. I'll tell everyone in town if you make me do this."

"You'll do nothing of the sort, Janie. This is killing your mother. You are killing her, do you hear me? Haven't you even thought about what this is going to do to the rest of your family? We won't be able to walk through town. It'll be a field mine of rumors everywhere we turn. The Parker family name will be ruined. What about that? Are you going to ruin your entire family because you can't keep your skirt down?"

Janie slid to the edge of the seat and stood between me and the doorframe. The rage building was palpable. For a split second, I considered she might hurt me. I mean, I wasn't a spring chicken anymore. I was pretty sure she could take me down. I just had to make sure she didn't know it. I straightened myself and left a space for her to get out.

Janie turned to face the security guard, who'd been watching us since we entered. Pervert. She turned back to the car, staring down at Charlotte, who still sat there useless and crying. I couldn't take much more, and opened her door as well, willing her to get a grip.

Across from the clinic, a small group of women stood hunched together and watched us intently. As we walked closer to the building, they opened their circle and spread out across the sidewalk. The tallest of the group, a lanky blond, held a sign that read: Life is a Choice. The woman beside her, a small brunette with an enormous pregnant belly raised an enlarged picture of a little girl with dark curled hair and bright blue eyes. Her picture sat under the caption: Changing My Mind was the Best Decision I Ever Made. The three other women held hands and lowered their heads in what I could only assume was a prayer. Fanatics.

As I pushed us toward the entry, an SUV passing by skidded as it slammed on its brakes. The smell of burning rubber filled the air. A big-boned woman with a heavy gait and spiked hair jumped out of her car and headed toward the protestors. This was gonna' be good.

"You think you can stop these people?" she screamed and flung her arms in our general direction. "You fools couldn't stop me! I've had seven abortions. It's my body. And, I'd do it again if I needed to. You bunch of self-righteous hypocrites." She rushed toward the tall blond and pulled her arm back as if she might punch her clear in the face. I heard Janie suck in a breath. From the side, the women circled again and raised their hands intermittently as the fervor of their prayers seemed to rise and fall to the beat of the woman's rant.

Crazy-spike was within inches of the blonde's face and right as I thought she might strike, she stopped—her mouth gaping open. It was as if she was ready to spout out another rampage but instead became dazed. Clearly on drugs. She pulled down the edge of her shirt, smoothed her spikes and rushed back to her car. A squeal erupted as she sped away.

Janie stood eyeing the brunette as she walked over to comfort the blonde. Her hand moved to her stomach and I knew we had to get this over with quick. Enough was enough.

Chapter Ten

Charlotte

Entering the clinic behind Purdy and Janie, I felt like a helpless bystander. I don't know what I was expecting as we came through that door, but I was shocked by the appearance just the same. Inside, it was decorated like any other doctor's office. But, it felt incredibly different. Wooden chairs covered in dark blue upholstery lined in a grid formation forcing patients to face each other. As if being inside a place like that wasn't difficult enough, they were made to look into the eyes of those who shared their fate. We were not like them.

Purdy marched to the check-in window as if she'd done it a thousand times. Janie stood to the side and tried to peer past the reception area into the clinic rooms. Money exchanged hands—a large amount of cash—and I knew Janie would soon realize she was not here to talk. The receptionist put a note inside a medical chart and my stomach churned. Janie's name was on a permanent record in an abortion clinic.

"Over here," Purdy snapped as we walked to the line of seats furthest from the front door. Janie, Purdy, and I sat in a row, in that order. Purdy held onto my hand and Janie's wrist as if either of us might make a break for it at any moment. In many ways, I hoped Janie would. But, those were the thoughts of a coward, of course. It would get me off of the hook. Even if she had done that and succeeded, it wouldn't stop. Purdy would never relent in her efforts to cleanse the family name.

Janie grew visibly agitated with each girl's name that was called. Women of every imaginable age and station in life filled the chairs, waiting to have their "problem" solved. I was so conflicted by it all. It was too early to call the child a baby, right? Or, even a child at all. Only a few weeks old, could it resemble anything even human?

"So, I was picking up some peaches at Lowry's stand yesterday and you would not believe who Marlin Waycross had with him in his car as he passed by—not his wife, I can tell you that much." Purdy glanced around as if this conversation might land on ears she didn't intend. Not likely.

"It wasn't Marcie? He has a sister, you know," I said as I rifled through my pocketbook with my free hand. I had to turn my phone off. I'd been avoiding talking to David and knew if he called in the middle of this catastrophe, he'd hear something in my voice. Something familiar maybe, that I couldn't chance. I pulled out my cell and hit what I hoped was the silencer.

"Well, of course not. Do you think I'd bring it up if he was riding with his sister? I'm not a total gossip. I don't make this stuff up, you know."

I tossed my cell back into my purse and turned toward Purdy. "Well then, who was it?"

"Well, I'm not saying it was Gertie Callahan, but a woman—who was an exact replica of Gertie in every possible way—was sitting right next to him. I mean, right next to him. Practically on his lap. I don't know if you've even seen her lately, but I'll tell you that woman is uglier than a mud fence in the rain."

"Do you think they were—" I asked, as Purdy dropped my hand giving me the freedom to search my pocketbook for a piece of cinnamon gum. I folded a piece into my mouth, and then offered one to Purdy.

"Really, Charlotte. Gum? How common are you?" Purdy asked.

"Are you kidding me?" Janie asked. "Are we seriously going to sit here and do this, like—like we're at the Magnolia Café over lunch or something? Do you realize where you are? I mean, surely you do. This was your idea, Purdy." She stared directly at Purdy.

"Oh, no. Don't blame this on me, Sunshine. This is your Mama's plan—tell her, Charlotte."

I was stunned silent. This was absolutely not my idea. It's just that, well . . . I didn't have any ideas at all about what to do. Which meant Purdy forced her own.

"Well? Tell me, Mama. Is this your idea? This is the scar you want to leave on your daughter's life? Tell me!"

I stared at Janie, unable to speak. What was I doing here? What was I letting Purdy do to my child?

"I hate you!" Janie yelled and yanked her arm away from Purdy, rising to stand.

"You sit your little behind down right this minute!" Purdy pushed through her taut, angry lips. "You are not going to be the end of my family's good name, Janie Johnston. Not you, or this bastard child."

I gasped and jerked my hand to cover it.

"This—what did you just say?" Janie asked in a way that scared me.

"You heard me. That's what you've done, you know. Have this baby and you sentence it to a life of shame as well. Ruin everyone's life. You think you know everything, little girl, but you don't know anything. You, my sweet niece, are a mere child. Now sit down like one and shut your mouth." Purdy jerked Janie's arm downward as she winced and sat beside her.

I couldn't believe Janie was going along. She'd always been such a fighter in our arguments. David bragged about her becoming a lawyer since Kindergarten. She refused to defer or admit defeat to anyone. Yet, here she was.

"My child is not something shameful." Janie growled as others in the room began to turn in her direction. I half expected them to jump on her side, as if they were all here by force. But, I knew from the amused look on their faces that most of them were comfortable with their decisions.

Before I formed you in the womb, I knew you . . .

The verse came into my mind in an abrupt moment, leaving me unsettled. A distant memory filled my senses. David and I sitting before the minister discussing our pending marriage. Though not a stranger to young marriages in that day, the pastor seemed quite disturbed to discover I was pregnant. It took him but a split second to bring those words to my attention. In what I'd thought would be another reprimand, his eyes were filled with gentleness toward our situation. Those words encouraged me through my pregnancy and the early years of my marriage. I hadn't thought of them in years.

For a moment, I almost forgot where I was. All of the eyes resting on Janie averted, except one. A young girl, much younger than Janie, sat in the opposite corner and watched Janie intently with what I swear seemed like longing. I wondered if she wanted to be here, or had been forced by a family bent on ideals as well.

Then, as if some sort of priority list existed for patients verging on a hissy fit, Janie's name was called.

"Janie Johnston?" A young black woman in a green hospital uniform stood at the door. Janie rose, followed by Purdy, then me.

"No!" Janie screamed at both of us. "You may have brought me here, but you will not—no, Purdy."

"Well, fine. I don't want to play any more a part in this disaster anyway."

The nurse interrupted, "You can't take anything with you back there."

Janie shoved her pocketbook into Purdy's middle, almost knocking her off her heels.

"Janie—do you want—" I started.

"I hate you," Janie stabbed and I felt my heart break in an instant.

God, help us all.

Chapter Eleven

Janie

I entered the long white hallway and followed the nurse without speaking. She pelted me with questions about my last period and what I'd eaten that day, but I didn't respond. My mind was racing as I surveyed my surroundings. Maybe I could find another exit. Maybe I really was here to talk. Maybe I could convince the doctor to make my family think I'd done what they wanted. We came to the end of the hall and turned into another doorway. The doorway to hell.

"Put this on, with the opening in the back," the nurse said barely acknowledging me. "You can leave on your socks and bra if you want to. Sit on the table when you're ready. The doctor will be in shortly." The nurse placed the items on a chair, rearranged my chart and laid it on the counter beside the doctor's swivel chair.

I opened it the moment she left. I had to know what kind of information Purdy had given them. Was Drew's name in there too? I tilted it open to find the entire folder comprised of one sheet. One. On it was my first and last name, a fake address, and the words "not applicable" written where my phone number should've been. For a split second, my heart eased a bit as I thought of Purdy protecting me. Then I realized, of course, that it wasn't me but the Parker's she would do anything to protect.

Footsteps in the hall made me aware that another patient was being pulled into a room. I wondered if they understood what was getting ready to happen, or if someone convinced them it was nothing. Or, maybe they too were being forced.

I didn't undress. I wasn't doing this thing they wanted. I sat on top of the pile of items in the chair and held my hands between my knees, rocking back and forth. The woman on the curb outside came to mind. She seemed familiar somehow. Then, I realized—the store owner. My mind raced to remember all the things she'd said to me. A gift from God? I laid my head in my hands and bent over my knees. God, please forgive me for what I've done. I'm so sorry if it's not what you wanted for me. But, please God, please don't take this out on my baby. Please help me save it. They don't need to know. They'll never know, if you'll get me out of here. Please.

I was more alert in that room than I'd ever been in my entire life. Every nerve in my body was electrified. I monitored every motion and noise outside the door, trying to get an image in my mind of how things might proceed. I sat alone for such a long time I wondered if they'd forgotten about me. Then, I heard a rustling in the hall and realized they were working the rooms in order. I would be next.

Down the hall, I heard the entrance from the waiting room open and a rushing of feet.

"You're not allowed back here. Wait for her in the waiting room."

I couldn't hear the mumbled response, but the door slammed shut and I could swear I heard a lock click. I wondered if the person was trying to convince one of these girls not to do this. If given the opportunity, would everyone be as eager to leave as I was?

I could hear a man talking in the room next to mine, but I couldn't make out his words. Still, I was certain it was the doctor. A muffled cry of a young girl made me nervous. I willed my mind to go blank, but all I could think about were the images of my baby I'd researched online. At eight weeks, it had distinct facial features, produced its own blood type and was starting to grow. I wondered what my blood type was. I poked around the room for information about anything related to the child inside me, but there was nothing there. They only spoke of clumps and cells.

A quiet rap on the door startled me, followed by a pause that made me consider trying to escape through the small window. Cracking the door open, a middle aged man eased his way into the room. Thin and balding, his glasses were entirely too small to be considered prescription reading glasses and I immediately concluded their sole purpose was to make him look more capable. He took them off and tucked them into his lab coat pocket where the title "Dr. Shields" was embroidered along the edge. I wondered if the clinic had a closet full of identical jackets so he could do a quick change between procedures.

Dr. Shields opened my chart and glared at me as if he knew it had been tampered with. I glanced at my shoes.

"So, Janie. Is there a reason you're not gowned?"

I sat silent. Lord, now, do something now. Please.

"Are we doing this procedure today, or not? I've got a busy schedule—"

The door flew open. "Dr. Shields! The patient in room seven—something's wrong—"

Dr. Shields leapt from the chair without any explanation, leaving the door wide open. A frantic stirring of nurses and office assistants bolted past me. I could hear a girl crying out in the room they surrounded as the doctor pushed his way through, slamming the door behind him.

I stood in the doorway unnoticed as those in the hallway whispered in hushed tones about hemorrhaging.

The door to the room opened and a nurse rushed toward the back door carrying a white trash can filled with bloodied gauze and a small bundle wrapped in white. The form of a small body took shape in my mind.

As the bystanders watched the emergency with riveted intensity, I started out of the room. Footsteps squeaked their way from the reception area toward me, and I held back a moment and let the receptionist pass. Then, quietly, I rushed down the hall and through the exit door where Mama and Purdy waited.

"Oh, thank God," Purdy said. "I thought you were the one with the emergency."

"Where's Mama?" I couldn't believe she'd brought me here and then left me with Purdy. Alone.

Purdy ignored my question. "Are you okay?"

I ignored her as well and walked out as quickly as I could without seeming suspicious. I held my hand over my stomach and slouched slightly as if I were sick.

Mama saw me coming toward the car and jumped out to meet me. "Is everything . . . okay?" she asked. She took my hand and slid her arm around my shoulder, trying to comfort me. A good girl like me, who did what her family asked, deserved comfort.

The thought sickened me and I pulled away from her on instinct. Mama kept coming along side me and rubbing my back and smoothing my hair as I got into the car. They never once questioned whether there was some sort of check out procedure. As much as I hated them that day, they seemed truly stunned at the thought of me actually going through with it. They followed my lead and it occurred to me they probably felt indebted in some way.

"You made the right choice, Janie," Purdy said.

I glared at her. You have no idea how right you are.

"It really is for the best, sweetheart," Purdy took on a tone I'd never heard in her voice before. It sounded like sincerity.

"Okay, now. Leave her alone, Purdy. This is all very traumatic. She needs to go home and rest. Do you want to stop at Ruby's and grab a milkshake, honey?"

I shook my head in disbelief that people could act so civilized over something so horrific. Mama took it as my answer, nodded to Purdy to crank the car, and we pulled out of the lot.

In the back seat, I slid my hand under my shirt to feel my baby.

* * *

Somehow I'd fallen asleep during the short ride home. I awoke with both arms wrapped around my middle, my purse open on the floor, and Purdy staring at me over the back seat. Purdy and Mama got out of the car and came around to my door as if I needed to be lifted out or something. I wasn't exactly sure of how I should pretend to feel, so I went along with whatever they offered. I knew I would need to check the internet for symptoms if I was really going to pull this off. I tried to open my door, again nothing. Purdy rushed to respond as Mama leered at her in anger and said, "Really, Purdy. That's totally unnecessary."

Zee was hiding in the bushes behind my house when we got home. He was the first thing I saw as I sat up, but paid him no mind. The thought of him knowing what they'd tried to do to me was more than I could bear. I wondered if his mama, Ms. Ellie, ever considered something like this when she was pregnant with him. But, I knew that couldn't be the case. She had a quiet strength about her—something ethereal—that seemed to get her through anything. I longed for the same.

"You go on up to your room, honey. I'll make you a little something to eat and bring you a magazine. You need to rest." Mama hovered beside me, urging me forward and blocking the space between me and Purdy. We entered the house through the garage and Mama turned abruptly at the top of the steps to whisper something I couldn't make out.

"Well, now you get a backbone." I heard Purdy mutter under her breath as she walked away.

The door closed and Mama faced me, but couldn't look me in the eye. "I'm going to run to the store, hon. Get you some of your favorites, okay? You rest. I'll be back in a minute."

I didn't respond and silence soon filled the house. After a moment, Mama sighed deeply, and turned to go back out through the garage. Would we ever be the same again?

I trudged up the stairs to my room, examining the mixed-matched frames that directed me upwards on a diagonal. My life splayed across the sage green wall. A picture of my first dance recital in an over-starched pink tutu, with knobby knees bent in a pose. A crooked angled photo of me peering up at Daddy as he snapped a quick shot of me blowing him a kiss, my face stretched upwards to reach him, his hand reaching down to touch my face. The mother-daughter-tea Mama and I'd gotten completely overdressed for the year I was a Daisy scout. Then, my senior high school picture in a black velvet scoop-neck blouse every senior girl was forced to wear, and Mama's wedding pearls. I touched the last one, feeling so far away from the girl in that picture. That girl had a lifetime to look forward to. The promise of so many good things. Was all of that gone for me now? If I stayed, it was only a matter of time before I was discovered.

I wondered now if I knew my mother at all. All the things she'd been so careful to teach me as I grew up. All the times we'd sat in church together as she explained how God felt about the things we were doing in our lives. I'd bought into everything I'd been told. Was it all a lie? Or just for show?

I pressed on toward my bedroom, brushing the tips of my fingers along the walls. The Parker's would disown me as soon as they discovered my secret, no doubt. One thing was becoming clear: once they knew, I would leave.

I'd been sitting on my bed for at least a half hour when a ruckus in the back yard pulled me to my window. I raised it and poked my head out to get a peek. Through the gaps in the old magnolia, I could see Zee running wildly through Purdy's backyard toting a BB gun.

"That idiot mother of yours. You're going to kill someone," Purdy yelled.

Lord? No, never mind. I'm sorry. I swatted my hand and grinned.

I pulled back as a mess of birds fled toward me from the magnolia's thick branches, indicating Purdy and Zee were headed my way. I hurried down the stairs, knowing where he would go.

Outside, Purdy flew by me in a rush, flowered house coat, hair in curlers and broom flailing wildly. I couldn't believe she'd gone home to get ready for some sort of social event after what had taken place this morning. Nothing was significant to her. Purdy paced back and forth as she lost sight of Zee and tried to locate his whereabouts. I stood to the side, inching backwards toward his hiding place to help guard any slip ups he might make.

"Well—what—the . . . where in the world? A grown man doesn't disappear . . . Janie! Did you see him?"

I shook my head and bit my lip to stifle a laugh. Mama pulled up in the driveway, her door jolting Purdy. I imagined her coming to the realization that she was out in public, in the middle of the day, without her face on. Her hands fled to her curlers and patted them down as she rushed through the carefully mowed back yards between our homes.

"Janie! What in the world are you doing out here? You need to be in bed."

I nodded in agreement. Zee caught my foot as I began to walk away.

"It's okay, Zee," I leaned down and patted his leg. "Game over. The witch is dead."

Zee crawled from beneath the steps and stood crouching beside the bushes, looking at me with a wide grin. I took him by the hand, and pulled him toward his yard as he began to swing our arms in unison.

He walked slowly. Slower than I'd ever seen him move. I pulled him forward as he pulled me back.

"Baby. Be careful. Mama said," Zee whispered as if keeping a secret. He had no idea he'd busted himself.

"I will, Zee. You need to stay out of Purdy's way. You be careful too."

He smiled, then placed his hand over his mouth, as if ashamed of something.

"Listen, I don't know what you've done to make her so mad. But, you need to make it better, okay? Just stay clear of her and give her some space. She likes her space."

He nodded slowly as we arrived at his back steps.

His mother, Ellie, stood watching the two of us from the window of her door. As we got closer, she came out to greet us, smiling. Her face soon changed however, as she saw me. I tried to brush the day behind me and hoped I could at least fool Ms. Ellie. Of course, that was hopeless. She knew me almost as well as my own mother, having practically raised me alongside Zee.

"Janie, what's wrong? You look . . . awful."

"Um . . . thanks, Ms. Ellie," I laughed hoping to play it off.

"Oh. I'm sorry. That is completely rude. I didn't mean it like that, hon. You just don't seem to be yourself. Is everything okay?"

"Yeah. Yes, ma'am. Everything's fine." I forced a smile willing my face not to betray me.

Ellie focused downward, as if saying a quick prayer. "Okay, then. I'll buy it for now. But, I want you to come and talk to me if you need to, okay? When you're ready."

"Okay," I said quietly, revealing something I'd hoped wouldn't be seen.

Zee took his mother's hand and went into the house. As I walked away, he tapped on the window waving goodbye. I waved at him with my foot, which made him laugh, and walked toward my house waggling my hips from side to side. I heard his muffled laugh and imagined his hands against his mouth as always, hiding from everyone but me.

Chapter Twelve

Purdy

Why people let their children run around like crazed lunatics was beyond me. It was only a matter of time before that boy was going to hurt someone—and it wasn't going to be me, or Tizzy. As if Ellie didn't have enough problems, she let that—Zee—track through my yard with a gun? Who did she think she was tampering with? I mean, that boy traipsed right through my hydrangeas of all things. Didn't he know how hard those were to grow in this sandy soil? He was getting on my very last nerve.

I stepped back inside, and hurried to check my hair to make sure none of the curlers had gotten out of place. One slanted curler and my whole coif would be a complete embarrassment. My family was going downhill fast and furious. I at least owed it to them to keep up appearances.

The fray in the backyard cost me at least twenty minutes. I couldn't be late going over to the Parker homestead to check on Daddy. He would throw a pure fit. But, my mind seemed to stop and lurch as I tried to pull myself together. All I could think about was what happened in that place in Malton. All of those wretched women. For some reason I couldn't really understand, Mother kept flashing to mind.

I must have been eight, or maybe nine years old. Old enough for Daddy to ask me to help, which I loved, and likely the reason I agreed. Mother laid in the backseat of Daddy's Buick, after he'd carried her out of the house in a rush and carefully placed her there. Charlotte wasn't with us, but that was nothing unusual. The worse Mother became, the more Granny Finn took charge. There was no one I wanted to be more alike than her. That woman knew how to maintain control.

I remember Mama lying on the leather seat, hunched together in a ball even though the seat was long enough to spread out. She was crying, and mumbling something about the time. I kept asking Daddy what was wrong. He kept telling me she'd eaten too many corn fritters, but I hadn't smelled any in the house— and I would have, they were my favorite. I just nodded my head at everything he said, hoping I might understand it later.

The next part was kind of blurred. A dash of red on the front of her dress. Daddy veering off the road into the gravel. Mama screaming out in such a terrifying voice that it haunted every dream I had for the next two years. I remember being told . . . something. To hold something. Yes. I crawled into the backseat and sat on the floorboard, holding a thick towel between Mama's legs while her eyes rolled back in her head. I've never been so afraid of someone in my entire life.

The car vibrated with every bump and rise in the road. My knees ached as I slid on them, the car careening from side to side as Daddy drove and watched us all at once. After what felt like hours, Daddy pulled abruptly to a halt. My head slammed against the seat and I dropped the towel, soaked completely with Mother's blood. A rush of men in white surrounded the car and I ducked hoping they wouldn't hurt me as they pulled Mother from the backseat flailing and crying.

A long and hollow siren screamed against the night sky, racing away. Daddy was breathless and crying, something I'd never seen in a man before. He slumped with his hands on his knees, head lowered, and faced the direction they'd taken Mother. In a sudden surge, he skitted to the edge of the road, leaned over and let go of everything he'd eaten that day.

All I could think to do was pray like Granny Finn would have. God, please don't let my baby brother die.

Chapter Thirteen

Charlotte

I placed the groceries near the pantry and stood there for a moment. I couldn't think straight. My mind spun with the images of the day. How could I lead my daughter to such a place? Like a lamb to the slaughter. What kind of mother allowed that? I could barely hold myself together, but I knew I had to for Janie's sake.

I wanted so badly to tell her I'd tried to stop it. The moment Purdy went to the bathroom, I'd tried to get to her, but the nurse cut me off. I'd stood on the other side of the door as the lock clicked, pangs of hopelessness shivering through my body. Purdy had reentered the room from the bathroom to find me out of my seat and patted the seat beside her sharply, as if I was a child. Instead, I'd rushed out to the car, telling her I needed air. Purdy rolled her eyes at me as I hurried out to search the side of the building for another way to get in.

The gate guard watched me intently as I walked the perimeter, nearing the back door and the trash receptacle. I panicked as his hand went to his hip and he yelled, "Hey! You can't be back there, lady! Don't make me come over there."

I continued to test the waters, pushing further back around the building. When I saw him locking the gate and leaving his post in my direction, I returned to the car. Throughout it all I couldn't stop my mind from screaming, calling me what I knew I truly was: a traitor to my own daughter. I bent over the car, trying to gather myself as something small and pink caught my eye. A tiny bootie lay beside the car, mocking me. I didn't want Janie to see such a thing, so I picked it up and put it in my pocketbook. The very touch of it made me cry and I realized at once what Janie had said earlier was true: this child had been my first grandbaby.

The thought made me shudder now. I tried to focus on the task in front of me, pulling the groceries from the bags and setting the ingredients for pecan bars on the island. Treats that were Janie's absolute favorite and the perfect answer to girl drama, boy problems, and late night studying. I stared at it all knowing how foolish it was to place what had happened in the same category.

I blended the butter and sugar then cracked the eggs. My eye was drawn to a red dot and I saw something I'd never seen in all of my years of baking. In one egg, a spot of blood? The images of a baby filled my mind.

My hands shook and I hurried to the bathroom suddenly sickened. I grabbed a hand towel from the closet and turned on the cold water.

Lord, help me. Are you trying to tell me something?

I splashed water over my cheeks as tears began falling. I buried my face in the towel, letting go of the sorrow I hadn't realized I was carrying. Like years of built up pain, pounding on me at once. I tried to keep my voice down, knowing Janie might return from taking Zee home at any minute, but the quiet shivering breaths seemed to fill every empty space of the house as I wept.

I smoothed my hair and pulled it into a low ponytail, then cleaned the black smudges under and around my eyes. I studied the dull reflection in the mirror. There used to be a light in my eyes. Where had it gone?

I barely recognized myself anymore. Everything I was, from my trendy hair style to my designer shoes, was swayed by the never ending Parker voices in my head. The boutique makeup smeared on my face was something I didn't even like to wear. It was Purdy's insistence I "set a higher standard" for the rest of the women we palled around with. My hair color had been changed so often to fit their recommendations, I couldn't remember the last time I'd seen my natural color. Were my auburn highlights under all that blonde, or had it darkened to a deep brunette over the years? My sculptured nails now seemed foreign to me, making me search my mind to imagine my hands without them. I felt like I was hiding in a shell I hadn't chosen. And, one I now wondered if I would ever outgrow and move on from.

God, I don't even know who I am anymore. Do you see me in here? Not that you would want to, after what I've done. Can you even forgive someone like—

The back screen door squeaked shut, ending my prayer. I wondered why I'd even bothered praying in the first place. Surely this was the dividing point in my life. The thing that finally pushed God away. I could hear Janie's soft footsteps in the kitchen. On the countertop by the sink, my cell began to sing "I Can't Get No Satisfaction". Purdy was calling again. I hoped Janie would ignore it. Instead, a knock fell on my bedroom door.

"Mama, your phone's ringing. It's Aunt Purdy. Do you want me to answer it?"

I opened the door, my bloodshot eyes forced downward. "No, sweetheart. Here, I'll call her back in a while," my voice cracked as I held my hand out and took the phone.

"Are you okay, Mama?" Janie asked in a voice so genuine, my heart broke from the irony. How could she care about a mother like me?

"Yes. I'm fine. Of course. I'm worried about you, though. Let's get you back to bed, okay? I'm going to make you some pecan bars, if you want."

Janie smiled. "Um . . . okay, thanks." She returned to the stairs, holding her stomach.

I remembered holding my own stomach in such a way, as Janie grew inside. The connection of hand to baby was all a pregnant mother could hold onto until the day the doctor placed the child in her arms. A day Janie would never see with her first child, thanks to me.

My cell rang again. Purdy.

"What?" I yelled.

"Well. How completely rude, Charlotte. First, you ignore my call, and then you bite my head off."

"I'm not in the mood, Purdy. What do you want?"

"Fine. I was calling about my niece, is all. Just wanted to check in on her. Can I talk to her?"

"You saw her in the yard, Purdy. She's as good as she can be, I guess. What do you really want?"

Purdy exhaled a long, overdramatic breath. "Okay. I need to borrow your lemon colored silk scarf. I have a date with Ed Thomas, the judge. He's taking me to an outdoor café and I don't want to get cold."

"No."

"No?"

"You heard me."

"Well, you little ingrate. I gave you that scarf. It's practically mine."

"You did not. Daddy gave it to me. For my birthday."

"You ninny. Who do you think told him what you wanted? He's a complete moron when it comes to shopping, Charlotte. I don't care if he is our daddy. You're all a bunch of helpless mor—"

"Finish it, Purdy. I know you want to."

Purdy remained silent.

74

"You can keep the scarf. I'll leave it on the patio. But understand this: it's the last thing of mine you will ever take." I ended the call.

Chapter Fourteen

Janie

I stayed alone in my room for the rest of the day and evening. When Mama brought the pecan bars up, I faked I was sleeping. Mama laid them on my dresser, kissing my head as she left. I spent the rest of the night going through my life's belongings, trying to find some semblance of the girl I used to be. Everything from my first tooth to my corsage at senior prom was tucked away in some crevice of my room.

I hadn't heard from Drew since the day before and realized he'd asked me if he could come over and I'd left him hanging. He probably thought I was mad at him. That explained why he hadn't called. I grabbed my cell.

He answered on the first ring.

"Hey, Drew. I'm so sorry I forgot to get back to you. My family's had a lot going on over here, long story."

"Yeah. Well, I called over there all morning. I finally had to call your Aunt Purdy to get the scoop. You should have told me, Janie."

My face grew hot. "You called . . . Purdy? Why?"

"Well, I tried talking to your mom. She just kept crying. I was worried about you. You never leave me waiting like that. Besides, Purdy called me first, which was totally weird. Not that I'm mad or anything, babe. I totally understand now. She explained what was going on. She's very worried about you too. She told me what happened at the um . . . doctor. Are you okay?"

As if. I couldn't believe he knew. But, at least it would give me an ally. "I'm fine. Have you told your parents?"

"No. Thank goodness. I mean, they would've been so upset over nothing, huh?"

Nothing?

"Janie? I hate this cell phone . . . Did I lose you? Don't get me wrong, babe. I would have come with you, if I'd known."

I was speechless. Did he know me at all?

"Man, that's it, isn't it? I'm a total jerk. I wish we could have just run off and taken care of it together, babe."

For a brief moment, I misunderstood him and thought he was talking about running away and getting married. I had a quick flash of us being together, raising our baby. I started to blurt out the truth I so desperately wanted him to hear. His baby was still alive. Then, it hit me. He was just like them. A life in exchange of convenience. My temper flared, "How can you say that? Didn't you have any feelings for your own child?"

"My? Whoa, Janie. You weren't even that far along yet. You did the right thing. Don't get so upset over it. It's done, okay? We can't raise a baby right now. Someday maybe . . ."

Hearing him say that made me sick. Someday. Like our baby had a choice of when it came into this world and maybe it could—oh, say—pick a better time. Drew was right about one thing: I had done the right thing.

The frenetic beeping of a horn sounded in the background at Drew's house, or wherever he was.

"Hey! What are you guys waiting for? Get in line!" The voice of another girl came closer to the phone with each word spoken.

"Are you—who is—where are you, Drew?"

"Oh. We're at a water park. Just some friends from high—hey—" his voiced drifted, laughing. "Sorry," he came back more serious. "We're getting ready to go back in. Can I call you later?"

The phone clicked before I could respond. I imagined some blond in a high ponytail with a pink and lime tankini playfully grabbing the phone from his hand and ending the call. Bright white zinc oxide probably streaked her perfect nose. I stood in front of my dresser mirror and wondered what I would look like in a bikini after the baby. Was I ready for this? Alone?

I had barely gotten off the phone with Drew when my cell rang again. I checked at the number, it seemed familiar, but wasn't in my address book so the name didn't pop up. I hated answering calls without caller ID. I hoped it was tankini-girl. I had a few things to say.

"Um . . . hello?"

"Janie? Is that you?" Purdy put on her sweet voice.

"Oh. It's you." I was annoyed. How did she even get my cell number? My mind flashed back to the clinic. She'd had my purse. There was no telling what Purdy had taken from my cell.

"Oh, well. How nice. I'm just so glad to hear your voice. Your mama wouldn't let me talk to you, sweetheart. And . . . well . . . I'm just worried about you is all."

Worried. Right. Worried I would tell someone what she'd tried to do.

"I'll be fine. I don't want to talk about it."

"Are you sure?" Purdy had a way of talking to you when she wanted her way, sweet and slow. Reeling you in because you thought someone with a voice like that must be the sweetest person on earth. Until the actual words came out. A skill many Southern women possessed, but Purdy perfected.

"You worry too much about me. I'm fine. Are you okay?" I didn't know what on earth possessed me to ask. Ingrained etiquette? I couldn't care less about how Purdy was after what she'd done. I hoped she was tormented, at the very least.

"Well, I guess I'm fine. I mean, I feel better now that I've gotten to speak with you. It's just that . . . I've been calling over there for the last hour. And . . . well, if you'd answered the phone earlier, I wouldn't have had to call the doctor over at the clinic to make certain everything went well."

I dropped the phone. It slid under my bed and I scrambled to pick it up. I could hear Purdy's voice the entire time, but missed whatever she was saying.

". . . beside that wouldn't really be your fault, now would it?"

Purdy paused long enough to hear me stumble over my own breath. A sure sign she'd gotten me. "I don't know what you mean, Purdy. But, everything is fine. You can leave me alone now." My heart raced.

"Oh. Is that right?"

I imagined Purdy's lips pursed as usual.

"So, you won't make time to talk to me, is that it? How completely rude, not to mention foolish, considering . . ."

She knew. Somehow Purdy knew. I racked my brain, searching what I remembered about privacy laws. Furious that someone at the clinic surely told her. That was the problem with small towns. They didn't have to follow rules.

Chapter Fifteen

Purdy

Girl, I looked good if I did say so myself. In fact, after getting ready, I had to go back and tone it down a bit lest Ed Thomas lose all control of himself. I mean, I'm not a hussy, and he was after all, just a man. I'd asked him to pick me up at Daddy's house for two reasons: one, Daddy loved that kind of thing even at this age; and two, after the day I'd had I just wanted to get out.

Daddy was dressed in a white button down dress shirt, khaki pants, and black knee-highs—the apparent dress code for elderly southern men. His body tilted against the couch, his fuzzy white head leaning to the side as he snored. I came in through the back door, and checked to see if the housekeeper had left his supper on the counter. Covered with a red striped towel, I peeked underneath to make sure she'd followed what I told her to do. Baked chicken with no skin, plain white rice, and a salad filled the plate, exactly as prescribed. He would be furious.

I'd recently caught on to his sneaky eating habits. Daddy had this way about him, sweet talking ladies into just about anything he wanted. The last time I'd checked on him, he was knuckle deep in a mess of barbeque ribs he'd convinced a neighbor-lady to bring over. He had no regard for what the doctor called "one scoop of meringue away from a heart attack."

"Daddy." I shook him. "Daddy, wake up, I want you to meet someone."

He opened one eye, closed it slowly, then jumped. "Oh, hey there, Darlin'. I'm so sorry. Did I fall asleep while you were talking?"

"No, Daddy. No. I just got here."

"Well, thank goodness. I'm not a total oaf, I guess."

"No, not at all. Ed Thomas is on his way over here to take me out. He mentioned wanting to meet you, so I told him to pick me up here."

"Well, sure, Darlin'. If it's important to you, it's important to me." Daddy reached to take my hand and patted it.

In the circle driveway, Ed's Mercedes pulled around, gleaming white from a fresh wash. Obviously, he knew how to treat a lady. I watched as he checked his teeth in the mirror and then brushed his pants off as he got out of the car. My heart fluttered at the sight of him.

He rang the doorbell and Daddy wobbled over to it, shooing me out of the room, offering me the chance of an entrance. There was something about Daddy—he just knew how I liked things to be. He was the only one who understood me at all.

I snuck down the hall to the bathroom, to check my hair once more. In the silence of waiting for my moment, a memory crept its way in.

Mother had locked herself in the bathroom again a few weeks after losing the baby. He was the first boy in the Parker line, beside Daddy, in three generations. I sat with my back pressed against the door, terrified. Daddy had gone with Granny Finn to take Charlotte in for a check-up and said I was plenty old enough to keep an eye on her. But, he was wrong.

Desperate to know what she was doing, I pressed my ear flat against the door and held my breath. I could hear her in there, messing in the cabinets. I racked my brain to think of what I'd seen in there earlier that morning: some Vaseline, a jar of face cream, a new toothbrush still in the wrapper from the dentist that had visited my school. She couldn't hurt herself with that, I figured. It was the soft bristle kind.

"Mother?" I asked in a loud whisper. "Open the door."

I could hear her crying quietly and talking to herself.

"Mother? Mama? It's okay. I'll take care of you if you open the door."

Her crying grew louder and I began to make out her words more clearly: "Just take me now, Lord. I can't bear it. I have nothing. I don't want to do this anymore."

We were going to end up in the hospital again.

"Mama, please. You have me, Mama. You have me. I'm not nothing." I begged through the door. I could hear a rattle of pills and I rushed to her bedside to see if the prescription the doctor had given her was still there. But it was gone, behind the door, with her. "Count me, Mama." I rattled the doorknob, pushing and pulling, hoping it would just fall to pieces. "Please! Come out. I don't want the Lord to take you away." I banged on that door until my fists were numb. I could hear the bottle tipping to the floor, the pills spilling against the tile, as Mother grew quiet. Crying through tears and anger, I curled up in a ball on the floor.

I wasn't enough for her.

A few days later I sat in the Parker pew at The First Church of Riverton, numb. Rows of people came and went, mumbling sorry's and what-a-shames. All of their eyes were on me, watching me, gauging my reaction. But, I didn't cry. I was too angry.

Charlotte, on the other hand, cried non-stop. She was still practically a baby and I don't know if she even realized what had happened. But, it was her cries that broke my heart. Her cries that willed me to get up every day after that. She began to choose me over Granny Finn. Likely, because everyone said I looked like Mother to her. I hated to hear that, but secretly relished that Charlotte refused to be comforted by anyone but me.

I soon became privy to the things only adults spoke of as Daddy, Granny Finn, and I talked about what we would tell people. Something like this would bring such shame to our family, they had reasoned. And so we lied. We would call it what it clearly wasn't: an accident. An improper mixing of the drugs Mother's doctor had prescribed to help her sleep after losing the baby.

We stayed to ourselves for a while, as families do when tragedy strikes. Plates of food, from overweight women in low cut dresses, were delivered around the clock. Women stopping their lives to console Daddy. I stood by his side at all times, refusing to budge lest I leave them a toe hold.

Soon, Granny Finn took over Mother's work, and life seemed to fall back into place. The house was quiet like never before and for the first time, I missed Mama's rants and non-stop chattering. All appeared well. And I pretended it was. And so my life became. The sole force pushing me forward was the fierce drive to protect Charlotte from all I'd known—to give her something better, a proper life.

Standing in Daddy's house that evening, listening as he and Ed made small talk, I realized too long had passed for an entrance. Now I was just being rude. I no longer felt like going out but I didn't want Daddy to see anything suspicious in my eyes. I floated into the room, my new lemon scarf flowing behind me.

"Well, just look at you." Ed whistled.

"You two don't stay out too late, you hear?" Daddy was playing up his part.

Ed and I peeked at each other and laughed.

"I'll take good care of her, Mr. Parker."

Daddy smiled and winked at me as Ed took my hand and pulled me through the door into a heavenly night. The dark sky, dense with stars, hovered over us like a canopy. Thin black chimney-sweeps swirled in pairs overhead, flying to their nests as the world quieted and settled in for the night. I wondered if I would ever feel quiet and settled.

Chapter Sixteen

Charlotte

I got up early on Sunday morning and took my coffee onto the patio as if it were any other day. I sat in one of the matching chaise lounges I'd recently purchased for me and David and stared out into the backyard. I knew I needed to tell him what was going on. I couldn't believe I'd been able to avoid him so far. I tried to enjoy the momentary solitude. The scent of vanilla mocha encircled my head as I scanned the rows of tulips that were beginning to bloom in my garden.

I hadn't slept in days. My nights were one long worry session. I was unable to stop myself from rewinding through the last days and trying out alternate endings than the one I had to live with now. I leaned against the headrest, closing my eyes. The sun warmed my face, though I felt guilty for even noticing. I longed for a vacation. Somewhere far away from here.

"Well, you're not going to get it done that way," Purdy yelled at me from across the neighbor's yards. She was going to wake them all. I put my finger to my lips to shush her, but I should've known better.

"What?! People who sleep late are plain lazy. There should be a law against it or something. It's totally gluttonous," she yelled as she closed the distance between us.

I shook my head, and laid back again, my hand pinching the tension building between my eyes. I tried to ignore her standing there.

"Are you going to get moving or not?" Purdy screeched again.

I had no idea of what she was talking about but watched as she gathered flowers and put them in vases. For the first time, I realized four of her vases were sitting on my patio. She began filling each one with pink and yellow roses. Then, she began cutting ivy as I watched, adding it to the arrangement. Purdy never put so much effort into something unless—then it hit me: Sunday lunch with the Parkers.

I had completely forgotten. The entire Parker clan would be there in a few hours, and I had nothing ready. I imagined my Aunt Flora prancing into the back yard to find it completely empty of the usual tables and finery I normally took pride in setting. Her grandchildren would whine about being hungry, and my cousin Nessie would smile, noting my failure on her internal calendar. I'd already spent two weeks cutting out pages in Southern Living and Better Homes and Gardens, trying to get ideas for spring tables. I'd even bought eight new silver mini lanterns I'd planned to place inside rings of fresh flowers. I couldn't believe a Parker event had slipped my mind.

My first thought was to cancel, but they would never let that slide. They'd be over, more nosey than ever, trying to discern why. My second thought was to tell the truth—but that was completely absurd. Not to mention, impossible with Daddy there. It would literally kill him.

I left Purdy in the yard and hurried to the freezer to see what I could possibly pull together for thirteen people who would be judging me with every bite. The remains of last year's vegetables Purdy, Flora, and I had put up, filled the freezer. It offered plenty of room for this year's harvest, but not nearly enough for a lunch that large. My mind was blank.

I walked to the bay window of the breakfast nook and stared at Purdy finishing up the vases. The crisp color of the sky caught my eye. A single puff of cloud was all that could be seen for miles. I suddenly had a deep yearning to go to church, not stay in the kitchen cooking. And though I normally skipped church on the Sunday's the Parkers visited, I didn't want to this time. But, there was no way I could do both.

I wandered to the buffet in the dining room and opened the silver drawer. Underneath the silverware tray, the edges of old take out menus peered at me. My favorite, worn and stained, fell to the floor: The Magnolia Café. I could call them and ask them to whip up something. It was homemade, kind of. Maybe the Parker's wouldn't even notice. And, it would give me the time I needed to prepare the table, make the sweet tea, and not worry about the food—plus, I could go to church. As long as I kept it simple. I'd just beg Marcie, the owner, not to tell anyone. That in itself would be a Sunday miracle since Marcie was second only to Purdy in gossip and rumors.

Marcie Green knew everything about everyone. Where they'd been, who they were with, and what objects they'd held in their hand. I often wondered if the Café was known more for its southern fare, or the undercover intelligence. If the FBI allowed crazed southern women as agents, she'd have been a prime candidate. Except for the top secret part. She'd never be able to handle that.

"It's a great day here at Magnolia Café, can I help you?" Marcie's drawl was always exaggerated.

"Marcie? Help! I need you to help me out this afternoon. It's Charlotte Johnston."

"My goodness, Charlotte. Is everything alright? The family okay?"

I imagined her with a notepad in hand, ready to take down the details of a scandal. "Um . . . yes. I'm sorry. I know this is very last minute. But, I've gotten myself in a mess. I um . . . burnt what I was planning to cook for Sunday lunch, and I'm just so embarrassed, I don't want anyone to know." It was so easy for me to lie, and I immediately felt bad about.

"Well, that's just fine, sweetie. It happens to the best of us. Is it just you, David and Janie?"

"No. I'm having the whole family over. Thirteen of us. I need you to help me get a meal together, but you can't breathe a word of it to anyone."

"Oh, now Darlin', really. Who would I tell?"

I could have named five hundred people, but I was desperate, and started rattling off a menu. The Parker's could just deal with it for once.

Chapter Seventeen

Janie

My head was pounding when I woke up on Sunday. I'd slept very little thanks to Purdy's phone call. The tangle of sheets and blankets on the floor were worse than usual. Each time I'd fallen asleep, I dreamed of Purdy doing something else to try to get rid of my baby. In one dream, I was tied to a chair, while Purdy dragged me into a room in her house that looked just like the clinic. In another, I was hidden in a closet, in labor, as Purdy talked to someone on the phone about giving the baby away. I rubbed my eyes and turned to the clock on the side table. A picture of Mama and me caught my eye.

I picked up the frame, one I'd made during Vacation Bible School using macaroni noodles and dried black-eyed-peas. Daddy had taken the shot, the two of us in sun hats. My pink hat was so big all you could see was my smile. Mama beamed at me with such joy in her face; I knew she loved me then. I missed her.

I was making my bed when Mama tapped on the door to see if I would join her in church. I missed sitting beside her on

Sunday's holding hands. But now, more often than not, I wondered why we'd even gone. Was it meaningless? I decided to take a chance anyway.

We pulled into the parking lot in Daddy's old rusted pickup truck. His Sunday beater, he called it. The truck always drew attention from onlookers and was something Mama never rode in, though today she didn't argue. I was officially nine weeks pregnant. My baby now had tiny earlobes, a mouth and nose. I felt like I was pudging even though I knew I still shouldn't show for a few more weeks. It seemed as if the entire world could tell I was pregnant.

The First Church of Riverton was the largest in town, something its members took pride in. The brick building loomed over Main Street, its stained glass windows throwing jagged shadows of color onto the sidewalk on sunny days. Inside, the cathedral ceilings were accented by flying buttresses joined in the center. Six tin-punched lamps, having said to be dated back to colonial days, lined the center aisle, guiding visitors forward.

I smoothed my linen dress, worried Purdy would comment on the wrinkles, though they were impossible to avoid. I held a white sweater over my stomach as I walked toward the building, suddenly conscious of the few extras pounds I'd gained.

An elderly couple, the Livingstons, stood at the wide wooden door and handed bulletins to those who entered the sanctuary. Mr. Livingston insisted on greeting each person by name, though he couldn't remember most of them.

"Good morning, Jessie. My, look at you all grown up right before my very eyes. What a beautiful young lady you've become." He shouted at decibel levels. "Isn't she lovely, Grace?" he yelled to his wife, who shared his fated loss.

"What? I can't move over any more, George. There is no space!"

Confusion swept across his face, and he turned to comment, but was quickly distracted by the next person in line, whose name he struggled to pinpoint. "Carl? Carl. It's Carl, right?"

I walked away as I heard Mrs. Livingston yelling, "The car? But, we just got here."

I tried to busy myself by looking over the Sunday bulletin, hoping doing so would give me an excuse not to socialize. Mama played the part of the perfect Parker, chatting endlessly about the older women's choice of hat, and remembering the exact dish they had brought to the last covered-dish lunch, that she desperately needed the recipe for. Though I knew such things were hard for Mama, she really had come to handle it with a refined flair that was impressive to watch.

Getting to the Parker pew took some maneuvering. Daddy stopped every few feet to speak to someone, pulling me over to say hello each time. As a deacon, he'd become a "stand-in" son to many of the elderly couples in the church whose families lived too far away to make a daily fuss over them. Most Sunday's he left with some sort of plumbing or landscaping task to look after for someone, and he'd come home later in the day with at least one plate of homemade goodies they had spent the afternoon baking for him.

"I'm sure I can make time for that this afternoon, Mr. Bryant. We planned a little family lunch right after church, but that will give me a good excuse to skip out," he'd said with a wink and a smile in Mama's direction. The Bryant's ate him up, and I smiled at the easy way people took to him.

The thought of the Parker lunch was something that had completely slipped my mind. Only a few days before, I had planned on explaining this all to them over lunch. Assuming that my talk with Mama went well, and she had forewarned them. I thought of the notes I'd scribbled on a piece of paper still tucked under my mattress. It seemed so easy then, to explain my choices away. Now, I had a new secret altogether. One they were dangerously tangled in whether they realized it or not.

Our small family usually sat on the outside aisle of the Parker pew. As if being a Johnston somehow lessened our rank. Grandpa Parker always took the first seat, closest to the main aisle, followed by my great Aunt Flora, Purdy, Mama, and Daddy, then me. Flora's daughter and her gang of rowdy boys usually sat on the pew behind us. The back of my head was a tempting target to five little savages who'd never once been scolded in their entire lives. My only saving grace was their daddy, Bud, whose broad shoulders and large hands could quickly sweep all five of them to the floor in one swift motion.

I was surprised this morning when Mama pushed Daddy ahead of her, to sit between her and Purdy. Purdy showed up moments later, noted the change in seating with a huff, and sat on her roost in the middle of the pew, saving seats.

"Mama, does she have to do that?" I asked completely embarrassed.

Mama turned to me and rolled her eyes. "Like anyone in their right mind would want to sit beside a rabid old woman, anyway."

I busted laughing out loud. Purdy turned, started to say something, then smiled sweetly instead.

Norma James came from the front side entrance and slid into her spot behind the organ. She threw her head back, glanced out at the crowd, then paused to appreciate the flower arrangements she'd placed on either side of the alter. As I followed her gaze, I swear I saw bacon in the bouquets. Bacon. Her creative flair never seemed to end. And though some of the older women in the church complained endlessly, the pastor let her do as she wanted, explaining that only God could inspire such unique ideas.

Purdy coughed as she apparently eyed Norma's latest offering, and my head leaned away from her on instinct. I couldn't bear to look in her direction even long enough to talk to Mama. In fact, I avoided contact with the entire Parker clan that hour; grateful for the two-parent buffer I'd been granted. I hoped Mama and Purdy were still fighting and hadn't talked since Purdy had discovered whatever she'd gleaned from the clinic.

Grandpa Parker and Flora finally arrived, smiling and nodding our way as they took their places. With the founding families in place, the sanctuary was starting to fill in with the remaining congregation. Occasional visitors gravitated toward spots in the middle, while newcomers scattered here and there trying to snatch a last minute seat.

It was always fascinating to watch how people reacted when someone sat on "their" pew. Some were gracious, and others were downright ugly about it. A young couple, the wife in the waddling stage of pregnancy, found a spot for two directly in front of Purdy in the McIver row. Justine McIver, a third generation member and the head of the membership committee, didn't seem as annoyed as Purdy would have been, and kindly slid down to make room, inquiring as to the couple's pending due date.

My stomach drew up in a knot as I eyed the woman with interest. I couldn't imagine myself getting to that point in my pregnancy. Would I have a cute little basketball pooch, like she did, or turn into a humongous blob? My hand moved to my stomach, as if on instinct. When Mama's head turned to notice, I winced a little—something I immediately felt guilty for doing.

To my far left, Purdy eyed me with interest as well, squinting one eye.

As the service neared the end, Norma James lifted her hands above the organ as if a cue to hush the crowd. Amazing Grace filled the sanctuary, and I choked back tears upon hearing the word "wretch". Certainly what I was.

Then, on the other side of the church, one pew up from the Parker's, something caught my eye. Maimie Cramer's shoulders shook as she bowed her head during the hymn. Others seemed to notice as well and within moments, heads touched together nodding and whispering in Maimie's direction.

Her head lifted, and she eyed the cross behind the altar. Then, she did something that never occurred at the First Church of Riverton—she stepped out of the pew. The whispers grew more nervous it seemed, as if someone walking toward the altar on Sunday was somehow shocking and disgraceful. I watched as Maimie knelt and Pastor Phillips laid his hand on her head.

I glanced down the Parker aisle where my parents, Grandpa Parker, Aunt Flora, and Purdy sat perfectly straight, perfectly dressed, perfectly smug, unmoved. Were we even here for the right reasons?

I'm a fake. Lord, help me. I'm a total fraud.

Beside me, Mama drew in a ragged breath. I peeked at her and could tell she was doing everything she could to keep from crying. Our eyes met, and both of us gave in, letting the tears fall.

Purdy pushed past Daddy, to sit beside Mama and pinched her hard on the back of her arm.

Mama flinched, then pushed Purdy away, drawing me into her.

"What in God's name are you doing, Charlotte? The entire town is here. Get a hold of yourself."

"I don't care, Purdy."

"You don't—what? Fine. I'll make an announcement right here then, spread your shame completely, if you don't care. . ."

"Fine," Mama said flatly. "Do what you want."

Then, in a Johnston move that would surely place a wedge between us and the Parker's for eternity, Mama and I stepped out of the pew and walked to the front to kneel beside Maimie.

Chapter Eighteen

Purdy

The Magnolia Café's catering van was parked on the street in front of Charlotte's house when we arrived home from church. Very interesting. I saw Charlotte bolt from her car and rush to meet Marcie with a check as David gathered aluminum pans filled with food from the rear van door. This was going to be fun.

"Talk about inconspicuous," I tried to get Flora's attention, but the old ninny was preoccupied with cleaning her coke-bottle glasses and couldn't have seen a freight train if it was running over her own feet.

Charlotte grabbed the two remaining pans and tip-toed across her front lawn, glancing our way to see if we'd noticed. A blindfolded imbecile could notice. Yet, here I was, stuck with the two most decrepit elders east of the Mississippi.

Like snails on muscle relaxers, we slowly made our way over to Charlotte's. We gave her a generous plenty of extra prep time, and yet she still wasn't ready when we finally arrived, eons later.

The smell of lemon dill chicken, hot potato salad, and asparagus filled the house as we entered. Janie quickly left the kitchen as we came in, carrying a pitcher of tea into the back yard. She was avoiding me.

Without greeting anyone, Charlotte stepped in line behind Janie, carrying the main entrees outside to place them on the long row of tables she'd set earlier. Three tables were covered in crisp white linen, stretching through the center of the backyard, a few feet away from Charlotte's garden. Shabby chic chair covers were tied with a bow, and appeared more like something a graceful wedding reception might boast, than a Sunday lunch with family. Candles of various heights and greenery flowed down the center of the tables, and four glass vases were filled with the perfectly arranged roses I'd delivered earlier. Ivy scattered among the centerpieces and wound around each vase, cradling them. I hated to admit how perfect it all looked. But, Charlotte did have her ways at times.

A warm breeze and the scent of a heavenly meal, beckoned the family to the backyard. I helped the elders come around and settle into two wrought iron garden seats closest to the house. Looking from the street, passersby might imagine the perfect Sunday lunch about to take place. The tension in Charlotte's face hinted otherwise. Our family was more like the Walton's with passive aggressive tendencies.

"Helloooo, Darlin'," Daddy hollered as soon as he saw Charlotte. Of course, she'd been standing there the entire time. Charlotte rushed to his side and kissed him on the cheek, mimicking the same greeting for Flora, but brushing me off completely. It occurred to me for the first time in a great while, the Parker's were not the massive clan we used to be. What had once been thirty or more, now could sit around a few meager tables.

Daddy squirmed in his seat, twisting every which way to see who was there and who we were waiting on. Nessie and Bud stumbled through the arbor near the driveway, their heinous little wretches following behind them, twisting arms, and smacking each other in the head. The twins, Jake and Jackson, followed by baby Hayden, and their sister Rachel. Rather than sit, Nessie let her evil spawn traipse all over the backyard, tearing through Charlotte's flower bed without a second glance. I saw Charlotte cringe, and didn't bother to help her.

David soon brought Daddy a tall glass of iced tea and they talked shop while the women gathered around the table, readying the food. In time, Charlotte had everything set and was forced to join us.

"Is it true, Char? I can't believe a word Purdy says." Nessie eyes gleamed with the newfound joy of a good piece of gossip.

"Yes, it probably is true. Not to mention, hateful. What did you hear?" Charlotte stared flatly at me, seething.

I stood strong, and rolled my eyes at her as if she was being too melodramatic. She hated that, of course.

"About—" Nessie lowered her voice to barely above a whisper. "About Janie. Tell me it's not true, Darlin'." Nessie looked genuinely disturbed, an impressive show of acting ability if you ask me.

"Yes," Charlotte sighed. "It's true. She was pregnant—"

"Pregnant! Oh my lord. Are you kidding me? You're kidding, right?"

Charlotte turned abruptly to face me, realizing she'd been tricked. I mean, seriously, would she ever learn?

"Well, what did you think it was? What did she tell you?"

"She told me she tried to run off and get married," Nessie stuttered. "She didn't tell me why. Good lord, it's a total rehash of history, is it not?" She took on a smug expression. Folding both hands over her mouth. Completely amused.

"Janie's her own person, Nessie. She's not me. And, besides, she's no longer pregnant. So, problem solved as far as you two wenches are concerned."

The men must have sensed a fit of epic proportions coming on. Within moments, they took their seats at the table, indicating lunch was to be served. Charlotte flitted past each seat, filling dishes and commenting on everyone's recent accomplishments. The picture of grace under pressure. I had to give it to her.

"Tell us about your plans, Darlin'." Daddy filled his mouth with chicken, and tipped his fork toward Janie, the object of his questioning.

Janie gave a desperate look in Charlotte's direction, and Charlotte watched as the rest of the table turned with interest. In a moment I couldn't pass up, I interrupted.

"Janie, Darlin'? Did I tell you who I ran into at the Piggly Wiggly yesterday?"

"No, who?" Janie asked, looking relieved. Charlotte watched me like a hawk, fearing what was to follow, no doubt.

"Lucy James. You know Lucy, don't you?"

"Of course she knows her, Purdy. The homecoming queen, the class president. Don't be ridiculous," Charlotte quipped.

"Well, anyway," I narrowed my eyes at Charlotte, "did you know she is in the pre-Med program at Duke? Yes she is. I tell you, some people just come up with a plan and stick with it. Not everyone, of course. But some can."

The comment infuriated Charlotte and she smacked a tea glass onto the table. The fact that Janie's hand moved to her stomach did not get past me.

"Wow," Janie offered. "That's really something. Her parents must be really proud."

"Well, of course they are—I mean . . . a doctor—can you imagine? That is really something special. Her mother is thrilled. I'm sure you can understand."

Janie's eyes avoided everyone, finally landing on her lap.

"Not that your mama isn't proud of you Darlin', you know she is. What's not to be proud of?"

A smug, satisfied smile spread slowly across Nessie's face and I knew if nothing else, she was enjoying the show. Charlotte rushed over and jerked me out of my seat, pulling me toward the flower shed like a reprimanded child.

"What are you doing?" Charlotte whispered.

"Oh, get over yourself, Charlotte. We're just trying to toughen her up a little. She's going to get a lot worse from the girls at school. We're just . . . helping her mentally prepare, is all. It's what we do."

"Well, stop it. I mean it. Daddy can't handle this right now. And, I can't handle him knowing. I'll tell him when I can bear to hear myself saying it without breaking down. Not today. And, have you forgotten David has no idea of what we've done? I can only pray he didn't catch what I said."

"You know, it's a miracle you even have a child. You're such a . . . a wus. And, if you don't tell David the truth, I will."

Charlotte eyed me then with an expression I can't even categorize. I'd clearly gone too far this time, and something in her changed. Not change in a dangerous way, like I should be afraid. But in a shutting down of sorts. I almost felt bad. She left me in the shed and took her seat at the table to finish the meal. She rushed us through, bringing out dessert and coffee before people had even finished their plates.

David must have sensed her urgency and began carrying dishes to the house as soon as everyone put their forks on the table. I fell in line behind him, determined I was going to wrap things up.

Obviously not seeing where I'd gone off to, Charlotte turned back to those seated at the table and tried to make small talk, smoothing over her behavior. If they could leave on a high note, she knew they would forgive the rest. She sat to Daddy's right and listened as he told Janie another story she'd heard a hundred times. Janie pretended to hang on every word.

From behind her, I helped David carry things into the house. This circus had been in town long enough. I was going to tell him come hell or high water.

I stood at the sink, my arms covered in suds up to my elbows. David stood to my right, learning against the dishwasher with a plate in his hand. I watched through the window as Charlotte began searching frantically from side-to-side. She found me through the kitchen window and our eyes locked.

You've never seen a woman clear a table so fast. Within nanoseconds she was loaded down with platters, bread baskets, and butter dishes, rushing toward the house. As she got to the door, she tried to readjust the plates and open the door with her elbow. She squinted as she peeked in and saw me leaning toward David as if I was going to whisper a secret.

Everything in her hands nearly dropped onto the patio and the entire Parker clan turned to watch as she squealed. Charlotte flung the door open at full force.

"It wasn't my idea, David! Purdy literally forced Janie to do it. I even tried to get to her. I swear I did. I'm just sick over it. I'm so sorry."

"Sick over what?" David inched away from me as if he knew what it was on instinct.

"The . . . the clinic?" Charlotte looked so confused.

David's faced turned completely white.

Chapter Nineteen

Charlotte

"How could you?" I screamed at Purdy so loudly, I barely recognized my own voice.

"I didn't. You did, and he needed to know anyway."

"Well, obviously, Purdy. And, I planned to tell him."

"Really? When? How long does it take to have a conversation with your own husband?"

My emotions boiled. She had gone too far. Again.

"It was my secret to tell, Purdy. Now, he's not only devastated, he thinks I was going to keep it from him."

"Well, obviously. Anyone with eyes can see that you were. I know you better than anyone, Charlotte. You had no plans to tell him."

The sound of my teeth gritting and the screaming obscenities in my head were all I could hear as I stared at the one person I hated most in the world. She had ruined everything. My relationship with Janie, and now my marriage.

Yet, I couldn't make myself say what I truly wanted to. I could only stand there, defeated and fuming, knowing Purdy had done exactly what she'd intended all along. As if the master puppeteer in my life, she synchronized everything I did, my life's acts to her own timing. She was the one controlling my life. And, I didn't even know why.

"Face it, Charlotte. It's better this way. Now it's out in the open. The two of you can get through it and move on. The family needs to put this behind them, for good."

I started to lash out at her again, and then stopped myself, wondering if she was right.

"Oh, good gravy." Purdy peered through the back window and rolled her eyes. "Someone should call social services on that woman and her child."

I moved closer to the window to see Zee in his back yard, with a hose. He held it in one hand creating a huge puddle beneath his feet, and smeared the resulting mud on his face with his other hand.

"He's completely harmless, Purdy. Why can't you leave him alone?"

"He's a pest. Like most children. Take a look at Nessie's rug rats out there. Did you see what they did to your flowers? Doesn't that bother you—oh—wonderful."

Purdy and I watched as the twins copied Zee by dragging a hose to the base of the steps where they were trying to create their own mud puddle to play in.

I walked out of the house, hearing Purdy huff behind me.

"Ya'll be careful there, now. Don't slip."

The twins smiled, dots of mud splashing against their legs.

Everyone else had moved to the garden. Daddy had his hand on Janie's back, leaning into her as she pointed out the various plants and flowers I'd recently planted. I was surprised to hear how much she knew about them, but even more surprised at the way the two of them were together. I paused at the edge of the garden for a moment, watching Daddy and feeling an odd memory struggle to come to mind. Something about the way he was handling her, protecting her middle almost, reminded me of years before. Right after David and I announced our pregnancy.

My heart raced. Did he know somehow? Maybe he'd overheard Nessie. Maybe he thought she was still pregnant.

I trudged over to them, deciding the day might as well be a complete disaster, and waited for the accusations to start.

"Charlotte, you really do have a gift for growing things," Flora said.

"Truly, Darlin', it's incredible what you can do with these roses. I've never seen such. Where in the world do you find them?" Daddy asked.

I had no desire for idle chit chat. I only wanted them all to leave. To get the fight over with and push them toward their cars. I was sure they could sense it, but wouldn't oblige me. "I cross-breed them myself, Daddy. Something I learned by accident, actually."

Daddy shifted his gaze from me to something behind me. In the furthest corner of the yard, Zee now stood, face smeared brown and wearing camouflage from head to toe. He carried something brown and slimy on a plate.

Janie had already spotted him and was quickly moving toward him, but tripped when Jake and Jackson rushed in front of her, covered in mud. Daddy caught her by the elbow, and pulled her arm into his—offering her his support.

Zee tip-toed through the back yard as if no one could see him.

"Mama, look. I think he thinks he's invisible," Janie giggled.

I watched in amusement as he went into stealth mode, slinking across the patio in full view of everyone. He stood to the side of the back door and peeked in. I could see Purdy hanging up the drying towel and opening the back door.

Zee placed his offering on the doormat and plastered himself against the wall, to blend.

Purdy flung the door open, surveyed the yard, and plastered a smile on her face as she came forward. Her first step hit the plate.

Her second, the air. Her foot, covered in the brown mush, slid clear off of the platter as she fell down the three steps and landed face first in the twin's mud pool.

The yard was completely silent. Then, Flora burst out laughing. A high-pitched, old lady laugh that sounded like the cackle of fairytales. Once she started, the rest of the family couldn't help themselves.

Fuming, Purdy stood up, glanced around at what could have possibly happened, and screamed at the top of her lungs for someone to do something. The entire family stared at her from the backyard with mouths hanging.

Purdy brushed her muddied pant suit, pushed her hands through her hair, and straightened herself. "Thank you, Charlotte, for a lovely meal," she clipped, mud dripping into her mouth. She spit to the side. The twins rushed by her pointing and giggling.

If I could have placed a camera on the scene and played it back in slow motion for the rest of my life, I still wouldn't have gotten enough. I watched as the monster drug herself back to her cave.

At the wall stood Zee. He glanced from side to side, and then tiptoed back to his own yard—unseen by the enemy.

I couldn't contain my smile.

Daddy came beside me, took my hand and squeezed it. "Some of the best things in life happen by accident," he whispered.

I turned to him stunned. He winked.

"Alright now, Charlotte doesn't want to babysit us all night. Move along, family. Let's get out of her hair."

I watched as Daddy gathered the family in a neat row. They followed him through the yard like ducklings being led to water. "It was a pleasure, Darlin'."

Standing in awe, I waved to the man I'd completely underestimated.

* * *

In our bedroom, David and I sat on opposite sides, though I longed for it to be otherwise. He wouldn't look me in the eye, but I could feel the anger seething, and it scared me.

"I was going to—"

"Don't." His teeth clenched.

"But, I need you to understand, David. I was still so upset by it all myself. I had to get my mind around it first . . ."

David glared at me and walked deliberately to the closet. He grabbed a small bag and threw it on the bed.

"What are you doing? Don't, David. You can't—"

"I can't? Why? Do you need to run it past your family first? Here, allow me." He picked up the phone and started dialing. I rushed to his side and hit the off button, taking it from his hands. "I thought so. You can't have it both ways, Charlotte."

"How is your leaving going to make this better?"

"Oh. I'm supposed to make it better? I thought that's what your family was for—cleaning up our 'messes'."

"It's not like that."

"Yes. It is. It's exactly like that. And, I'm completely sick of it. I mean, honestly, Charlotte, where does your loyalty lie?"

"With you." I paused, stumped by what to say. "Of course."

"Very convincing." David went to his closet and pulled a couple of shirts and pairs of pants.

My heart broke. I couldn't believe this was happening. I went to him, trying to put my arms around him.

He jerked. "Don't."

"David, please."

He stopped for a moment, his eye softening as he gazed at me. "Charlotte, I don't like what's happened to our family. I don't like that things are going on that I don't even know about. I don't like that you're hiding life threatening information from me about our daughter. I thought we were closer than that."

"We are," I pleaded. "Our family is so all encompassing. They want to be involved with every aspect of what we do. Especially

Purdy. Which, I know is nerve racking, but she doesn't have anyone. I feel sorry for her in a way—"

"Stop." His face reddened and he turned from me.

"What did I say now?"

"When I say family, I mean us, Charlotte. You, me and Janie. That's it. But, all you ever hear is 'The Parkers'. They are not our family. This is our family. They're just . . . a bonus, I guess."

He moved into the master bath and I could hear him loading his shaving kit. I sank into a chair. He was right.

He tossed the kit on the bed, then stopped at his nightstand and picked up his Bible. The worn pages flowed open, fanning as he held it to reveal the bits of blue handwriting in the margin. He touched the top of the Bible and closed his eyes for a moment, then turned to me.

"Your priorities aren't straight, Charlotte. Jesus first. Others second. Yourself last."

"I do put others before me. I'm always last. Even you say so. You're always telling me it's to my own detriment."

"Yeah, you do. The problem is, God isn't even in the picture. Because if He was, you'd see more clearly who the 'others' should be. I want us to follow Christ as a family, Charlotte. Not, 'The Parkers'.'"

Though I tried to think of the right words to say, my mind swirled with questions and uncertainty. I watched David watching me, a longing in his eyes that I say the right thing. If only I knew what that was.

"Just as I thought," he said. "I wouldn't expect anything less from a Parker."

Chapter Twenty

Janie

Monday morning arrived and with it, the fog. My mind felt oddly similar. As was often the case in early spring, the roads were covered in the warm, thick substance that made me long for summertime all the more. I slipped out of the house early, not knowing where I would go, but preferring to take my chances over the company at home. I'd managed to spend the rest of the evening in hiding, as Mama and Daddy fought endlessly downstairs. Surprisingly, sleep found me easily. I was completely exhausted, though I couldn't understand why.

I got into my car and tried to decide my next move. Pulling my seat belt in front of me, I pictured my belly getting larger and wondered if you were allowed to drive a car once you got really big. My hand moved slowly over my stomach in a round motion that somehow made me feel better.

As my car rolled out of the driveway, I noticed Mama at the window, a worried look on her face. I ignored her and pretended to talk on my cell so it would appear as if everything was getting back to normal. Of course it wasn't. And, I was sure it never would be again. I was unmarried and pregnant. Carrying a child my family hated.

What was I doing?

Meandering my car through the streets in town, I hoped to clear my head. The stores were laden with graduation items and signs of spring. I passed by the children's shop from the days before and saw the shop owner standing in her front window, creating a new Easter display. Cut paper flowers and grass wiggled along the base of the stand between stuffed ducks and furry bunnies piled in pyramids. She was wrangling a pair of oversized tulips when she stopped and turned, looking directly at me as I scooted by.

I snapped straight ahead, hoping she didn't really see me and then pulled my car into a nearby parking spot behind another car when I noticed the owner had left its trunk cracked open. I wanted to get out and shut it for them, but sat staring ahead. Unsure of why I'd even come in this direction, I laid my head on the steering wheel and sighed.

What am I supposed to do now, God?

The clip-clip-clip of high heels on concrete drew closer to my car and I kept my head low, turning to the side. The shop owner came around to the car in front of me, pulled a massive two-story gingerbread Easter house from the trunk and stood straddling it, trying to keep it from tipping over.

"Oh. Oooh." She squealed as the pink and purple mansion slid from side to side as if they were both on ice and trying to balance.

I couldn't let her fail. I reluctantly opened my door and rushed to the fender as the roof slid in my direction. Together, we kept it from crashing into the street.

"Well, my goodness. I mean, thank goodness. Thank goodness for you, honey. We can't let this whole thing fall apart, now can we?"

I smiled in reply.

"Hey! I know you. Don't I? I mean, I've seen you before, right? In my store?"

I shook my head but couldn't speak.

"Yes. I remember. And . . . oh. Yes."

I imagined her visualizing me at the clinic. I'd seen her with the sign.

"I know exactly who you are now. You okay, honey?"

I started crying. Again. What was it with this woman?

"Oh, now then. Don't. It's okay. Come on, help me inside with this. We can talk."

I closed her trunk and noticed the rear window was filled with the longest line of little stick people stickers I'd ever seen: one Mom, one Dad, and a windshield full of stick boys and girls. In the back seat sat boxes overflowing with children's clothes.

"Wow. Big family?" I asked.

"Girl, you have no idea."

We carried the enchanting little home toward the shop. I tried not to lean it on top of the woman's bulging belly while guiding her in the right direction and keeping it from toppling to one side or the other. She'd left her shop door open and we were able to ease it through and deposit it right in the midst of her spring window theme. I stood back and admired the details.

Icing was piped along the roof in scalloped edges. Hundreds of tiny round colored candies littered the icing grass as if hidden and ready for an egg hunt. Marshmallows dipped in green chocolate stood at attention along the edges of the home creating plump little bushes against the manicured lawn. I would have loved to have seen that when I was a little girl.

"Did you do this yourself?" I asked.

"Well, actually, yes. But don't tell anyone. I don't want them thinking I'm willing to do another. That thing took nearly three weeks. It looks delicious, but everything on it is stale as cardboard by now, I'm sure." She smiled and tilted her head toward me, looking to the floor and then returning to her gaze. "I believe . . . I saw you this weekend, didn't I?"

"Yes." My eyes fell to the floor as I struggled to hold back the memory.

"Well, I'm sorry. I wish I could've helped you more the first time you were sent here. I should have done more, I guess. I'm really sorry."

Sent there? "I. You did. I mean. I didn't. This weekend. I didn't do it. They made me go. They think I went through—" I stumbled over my words, not knowing how to explain it or if I should tell anyone this close to where I lived. I stopped midsentence, suddenly suspicious of her.

"What do you mean you didn't do it? You were in there an awful long time. You didn't go through with the, um, procedure?"

"No, I—"

"No? Did you say no?" She wouldn't let me get a word in.

"Yes. I mean, no. No. I didn't go through with it."

"I knew it!" She squealed another high-pitched noise that made me start to wonder if she was the kind of adult I should even be talking to. She seemed impish and playful all at once. "Well, that is just the best news I've heard this year," she said slapping her hands together and pulling them up to cover her mouth. It didn't stop the talking. "This is wonderful. Just fabulous. I can't wait to tell my support group. They will be thrilled." She stopped cold noting my stunned look. "Oh. Not to worry. We never share names. I've never mentioned to them that you were even in my shop. We were praying so hard for you as you walked through those doors. It was an answer to prayer. A pure answer to prayer," she beamed.

"Well, I'm glad someone's prayers are being heard, I guess." I leaned against the window frame and rested my hand on my stomach. The shop owner's eyes followed.

"And, I'm Gabby, by the way."

"Oh. Sorry. I'm Janie."

"I suspect yours are being answered too, Janie." She winked at me. "Whether you can see that or not."

I smiled, not sure how to react to that. "I'm not so sure about that. I'm pretty alone, actually."

"No, you're not. He still loves you. He won't leave you, Janie."

For a moment, I pictured Drew as she spoke. The two of us working this out. Then, I realized who Gabby meant. My heart sunk at the thought of what was happening with Drew, but at the same time, I wondered about a God who could love someone like me.

Chapter Twenty-One

Purdy

Oh, it was on. That little nuisance had pushed me too far. My new suit was completely ruined. Completely. The cleaners had taken one look at it and then laughed in my face. I couldn't believe I was the spectacle at a lunch planned to center around what was going on with Janie. She was not getting off the hook that easy.

I hightailed it over to Daddy's the very next day. He had to know. I mean, not telling him would be the same as lying to him. And, I did not lie to my Daddy. Much.

He was sitting on the front porch as I pulled up to the homestead. He wore a boater hat, tilted slightly, and sipped tea as if he hadn't a care in the world. A second glass sat on the table beside him and I wondered who on earth was there with him. A tinge of jealousy flared inside me.

"Hey there, Darlin'," Daddy stood, waving his hand to the chair beside him. "I figured you'd be here sooner or later."

The glass of tea was watered down now, the heavy amber color floated to the bottom leaving the clear liquid that once was ice layered on top. "How long have you been out here?" I asked.

"Pretty much all morning. I knew you'd stop by at some time."

"Well, what in the world? Why didn't you just call if we needed to talk?"

Daddy smiled, took my hand, and focused on my eyes. "Sometimes, it's better when we come on our own, is all."

I had no idea what he was talking about and somehow felt like I'd been reprimanded. "Daddy, you're making me feel like a child. Why are you speaking in code?"

He laughed. "It's not code, Darlin'. Just the truth is all. That's pretty much what I've been figuring out on my own. Though, if you'd like to add anything, feel free."

Did he already know? How on earth? Surely Charlotte hadn't gotten the gumption to prance her little tail over here and spill the beans. Janie? David?

"Well, you look like you've just seen a ghost, Purdy. I at least hope it's your Mama, if that's the case."

Mother. She'd been on my mind so much lately. All the secrets. All the lies. Somehow tangled together with the week's events. "Well, not that I've seen her, but I can't stop thinking about her lately, Daddy. Do you ever think about all of that?"

"Every day, of course. I miss her terribly. You should know that."

"I guess I do. But, honestly Daddy, even now, I wonder if what happened wasn't for the best. For the family, I mean."

Daddy stopped his rocker. He straightened his hat, and turned to face me. "Purdy, I want you to know what happened all those years ago, with your Mama, was heart wrenching for me. And, as such, I didn't handle it the right way. I was a young man then. A very young man, full of anger, and disappointment, and grief. But, I've made my peace with it. I had to. And, I'm ashamed to say I didn't make sure you'd done the same."

"I've made peace . . . in my own way. I don't hate her anymore."

"I'm not talking about peace with her, Purdy. I'm talking about peace with what you lost. Peace with not having the mother you wanted. Peace with living in an imperfect family."

For heaven's sake. Was he turning into a babbling lunatic as well? What was all this? I was at peace. I was at peace!

He took my hand in his, squeezing it, and I noticed age had changed them. They were no longer the strong hands that protected me from everything I feared. They were simply the hands of an old man. Weak. Spotted. Flawed.

"I can see I've upset you, Darlin'. And, that wasn't my intention. But, I'm still your Daddy, and I want you to know one thing." He paused for a moment and waited until I looked directly at him. "You need to move on. You can't control us any more than you could control what happened with your mother. People are messes. They make mistakes. They do bad things. Then, you choose to love them anyway. I hope you understand."

I shook my head as I rose from the rocker. I understood alright. He'd clearly lost his edge.

Chapter Twenty-two

Charlotte

The next morning, I found myself at the grocery store. I had no intention of going there when I'd left the house. I couldn't even remember getting there. But, as if on autopilot, I'd ended up at the place I most frequented. My mind was full of scenarios of what David might do now that he knew. Purdy's voice echoed in my head along with the horrific look on David's face when he'd found out about the abortion. Our last conversation stayed in my mind as if on replay, taunting me.

The tension between my eyes intensified and I wondered if it was the stress or the unbearable pollen that now coated everything in sight. The whole town of Riverton seemed to be tinted yellow, covered in the overzealous granules of spring.

I pulled into a spot in the front and laid my head back on the seat rest, closing my eyes.

What now, Lord? Is this . . . unforgivable?

An image of me and David as a young couple sitting on cardboard boxes flickered through my mind. We were eating our first meal in our new home. A nice meal. Maybe a nice meal of his favorite things would help ease his anger now? I'd done that often in the early years of our marriage. A tiff would arise over the baby, or something that had happened at the store, and somehow having a nice meal at the end of a bad day made all the difference to him. The idea seemed insulting now. I couldn't think of another time in our relationship I'd shown such betrayal. He was right about me. And my family.

I took my time through the store, a luxury I didn't usually allow myself. But, who was waiting for me now? I stopped at the olive station and taste-tested the spreads displayed on sample trays. Beyond that, I rolled to the back end of the wine aisle, noting how many varieties they now carried from David's favorite winery and picked up a bottle of red. I even stopped at the coffee bar and ordered a tall iced vanilla macchiato. "Double shot, please." I was determined to talk to David about this as soon as he came home. If he came home.

I browsed the meat section, eyeing a nice rack of lamb the butcher displayed in his window, David's favorite. I had no idea how to cook such a thing, but would figure it out somehow. I had a shelf full of cookbooks Mama had left behind when she died. Purdy had no interest in them, so they became a special treasure of mine. Cooking was the one thing I did that made me feel close to Mama, and feel like a good mother myself—laughable now. But, surely one of the worn books held a recipe. I stood staring at the marbled meats, missing my own mother more than I had in years.

God, I needed someone to talk to.

"What can I get for you, ma'am?"

I barely glanced up as I pointed to the lamb, but the butcher's eye was on another customer to my left.

"How's the salmon this week, Richard?" Maimie Cramer leaned over the counter, trying to get a look around me as I blocked her view. "Oh, Charlotte . . . Hi." Maimie's face blushed instantly.

116

"Oh. I'm so sorry. I didn't realize you were behind me, Maimie. I'm completely rude. I'm in a total fog today."

Maimie nodded, darting her eyes elsewhere.

"How's your son?" I asked, then noticed a flash in Maimie's eye. Almost like a look of fear.

"He's fine. Thank you. Um. Never mind, Richard. I think I'll stick with the chicken this week." She nodded to me and briskly moved away.

I watched her turn down the next aisle, glancing back toward me as she moved away. The Parker girls had a reputation. One I had never thought to distance myself from before now. I knew Maimie would expect no less of me than she would of Purdy.

"And, you, Mrs. Johnston?" Richard inquired.

"Um. Nothing. Thank you," I said, uncomfortable for the first time in my life that everyone around me knew exactly who I was.

I hurried down the same path Maimie had escaped through, but saw no sign of her. I abandoned my cart and it's belongings after the next two aisles, looking down each with no luck. At the next turn, I maneuvered past the check-out stands and found Maimie, cowering behind the register and quickly trying to pay her bill. She spotted me as she grabbed her bags and rushed toward the door.

Was I really that horrible?

"Maimie, wait!" I called, but it only served to hurry her further. I moved through the line of people, squeezing between carts and children begging for a treat. A little girl bumped into me and dropped her sucker, howling as I passed. I slowed at the automatic door, waiting for it to reopen. Maimie was already near her car, hitting her key chain button to pop the trunk.

"Please, Maimie. I just want—" I stopped short as my pocketbook fell from my shoulder and spilled its contents into the drive through pick-up lane. As I bent to pick up my things, I forgot about the coffee cup in my hand and tilted it too far, causing it to pour down the front of my skirt. Trying to correct myself, I squeezed the cup, as whipped cream and coffee colored ice cubes tinkled out and bounced against the blacktop. Tears began falling. My life's 'necessities': a Prada wallet and matching check book, Chanel pressed powder, and a tip calculator were displayed for the world to see. Among them, a small pink bootie, like a lit flare, flashing.

The bag-boy waiting to load the next car bent to help me saying, "Hey. It's okay, ma'am. No need to cry." He motioned to another worker to gather something to clean up the mess, and tried to console me with his charm. But I knew he had no idea from looking at me I wasn't the pulled together, perfect southern lady I pretended to be. I was so far from that. As far as I'd ever been in my life.

I sat back on the curb, like a defeated child, with my knees touching and my ankles angled away. I watched as the bag-boy picked up my things and gave no care to whoever saw me or whatever car was next in line to get their groceries. I was spent.

"Here, let me help you up," Maimie stood beside me, her hand outstretched.

"Are—are you sure? I totally understand if—"

"I'm sure. Up you go." Maimie lifted me off of the curb and out of my daze. She brushed off the back of my dress, blotted the front stain with a Kleenex, and tried to help me put my hair back in place. "You look—just awful," she said and then laughed.

"You should see the inside of me," I said, then joined in her laughter.

"Well, that's something I never thought we'd share in common. We'll have to take a good look at that, won't we? Come on, I know just the place." Maimie put her arm in mine and pulled me along. For the first time in a long time, I didn't mind being led by someone stronger.

* * *

"So, I noticed you in church the other morning," Maimie commented over a cup of coffee at the scariest dive I'd ever been in.

"Yeah. You too," I smiled. "I'm pretty sure the entire congregation had us labeled as fanatics by lunchtime. You're a real trail blazer." I winked.

"I was praying for Justin," Maimie said, her face growing more serious. "I'm so worried about him; it's all I know to do anymore. I don't care what anyone thinks. They're going to talk no matter what happens at this point."

"Is it working? The praying, I mean?"

"I don't know. I mean, yes. I'm pretty sure it is. Except I haven't seen how yet. I think God is working on him, though. That's all that matters. Justin's been asking me a lot of questions lately. I do the best I can to answer him without alienating him. I can only do my part, and God will do His."

I stared into my mug, pouring a little plastic cup of half-and-half then swirling it slowly with a spoon I'd noticed was less than perfectly clean. Still, it was definitely the ideal place to talk. Beside the two of us, the place was seated mostly with truckers and bikers, with an occasional couple scattered here and there. Even they seemed as if they'd just woken up and I imagined them walking over from the dilapidated motel next door.

Coffee stains patterned the linoleum floor as well as the Formica tables. The curtains were sun faded and appeared as if they had been hung the day the original doors opened however many decades ago. Still, people kept to themselves, save the waitresses who couldn't keep from looking our way. We were the misfits, something I found strangely comforting. The ladies from the club wouldn't be caught dead in such a place, and I wondered how in the world Maimie had come upon it.

The waitress stopped by the table, dropping off a full pot of coffee as if she knew we'd need it. Her arms were covered in tattoos. "Let me know if you, um, ladies, need anything else," her gruff voice bore witness to the cigarettes that peeked out over her pocket. She placed her pen behind her ear and as she walked away I noticed the dotted line of piercings that created an outline.

In a lower voice, I asked, "What if . . . if we don't do our parts? What then? I mean, what does He do with a mother like that?" Tears stung my eyes.

Maimie reached across the table and took my hand. "He does His anyway."

I lowered my eyes and my shoulders started shaking as tears began to fall. "I hope you're right. I really do. I'm the most horrible mother, Maimie. You can't even imagine how bad. And, I just . . . don't want Janie to pay for that. She's paid for enough."

"You're not a horrible mother, Charlotte."

"Yes, I am—you have no idea—I'm awful. Truly."

"I said I saw you on Sunday. Up there with her. In our church. I don't know what's going on with you, but I could tell she was leaning on you. That's something. I pray that Justin leans on me. He's just so . . . headstrong. He thinks he has all the answers. He won't listen to anyone—especially me."

"Funny. You wish your son would listen to you, and I wish my daughter hadn't listened to me." I put my head in my hands and let out a deep sigh. When I lifted up to see Maimie looking so genuinely concerned for me, I shared my story. The entire thing. Even knowing Maimie had the power, and a good reason, to share it with the vipers at ladies lunch on Monday.

It occurred to me then, it was Monday. In fact, I should have been getting ready to go over to the club right then. Instead, I was sitting in a truck stop. Purdy would have a stroke. And, for once, I didn't care.

"If you're truly sorry about what happened, Charlotte, make that clear. It sounds like you have some conversations that need to take place."

I glimpsed out across the parking lot toward the sky. Spotty clouds covered the area and a light rain began to fall, even though the sun still shone. I watched as the yellow dust of pollen that covered everything within eyesight began to gently wash away. A clean slate. Another chance.

"What if He doesn't—turn it around. What if He doesn't . . . forgive me?"

Maimie smiled and placed her hand over mine once more. "That's the thing you don't realize you have in common with Him. He loves His children too much not to."

Maimie slid out of her seat and pushed me over with her hip as she slipped in beside me on the other side of the table. "Make no mistake, Charlotte. He's in control. Whether you can see that or not."

In control. I mused that nothing seemed in control these days. Not by me, anyway. I had to admit, the idea was appealing.

"We praying mamas need to stick together, you know. It's not easy walking around with a target on your forehead, alone." She winked.

I smiled. Then, for the first time in years, I leaned my head on another woman's shoulder and trusted I was safe there.

Chapter Twenty-three

Janie

Sunday lunch with the Parker's had gone way better than I ever expected. But, I knew I was still being watched. Somewhere along the way, the tabs they kept on Mama had trickled down to me. Being her daughter, coupled with my Daddy's evil Johnston genes, left a gaggle of Parkers to fawn over my every hiccup in life. I have to admit I enjoyed such power in the beginning—doing things to make them worry and fret—but now I realized it was the one thing I longed to get away from most. The pressure of perfection was too much for someone like me.

I desperately needed to talk to Drew. I knew where my family stood, and was beginning to get a stronger footing on things, but he was the one missing piece of the decisions that needed to be made going forward. The baby I carried was his child too. Up to that point, I'd made all the decisions, even if everyone else believed otherwise. Even if he didn't want it, he had a right to know, right?

Daddy had not been home since lunchtime the day before and I knew he must have figured out what was going on. With everyone so distracted, I decided to call Drew and ask him to come over and talk. He arrived a few hours later in a brand new Honda I'd never seen before.

"Isn't it great?" He smiled broadly as he got out of the driver's side onto the curb and held out his hands, like a model displaying wares. "My mom and dad totally surprised me with it. Pretty cool, huh?" He was wearing my favorite tee shirt. The one I'd carried home and slept in the first night we'd spent together. It was worn in all the right places, as were his jeans—which made him nearly irresistible to me. His blond hair had gotten longer in the short time we'd been apart. Watching him made me think of surfing and the summer we'd planned together looming before us. His green eyes shone with excitement, and he winked at me not realizing how hard he was making it.

"Wow," I said, really commenting more on him than the car.

"I know, right? It's going to be great. A new car. Our summer at the beach. I can't wait." He strode over to me in the lanky walk of a boy verging on manhood. I envisioned us together, years down the road, living in the suburbs and raising our child.

"Yeah," I glanced down at my feet, not really wanting to be there, in that conversation.

He leaned in to kiss my cheek. He wrapped his arm around my waist as he pulled me toward him, his hand rising up slowly. He somehow felt so much freer to touch me now, since we'd been together. Like having sex with him gave him permission to do whatever he wanted to with my body now.

After two years of being together, I suddenly no longer knew how to handle myself around him. Everything we did now felt awkward and I was constantly worried he was looking at me— differently than he had looked at me before. It was so obvious now that we'd never been ready for the way our relationship progressed. Especially considering the final outcome.

"You okay, babe? I know you're still struggling with everything. It's written all over your face."

"I guess I'm okay," my mind skitted back and forth between telling him and not. "Drew?"

"Yeah?"

"I need to ask you . . . What would've happened if I hadn't gone along with Mama and Purdy? If I was still pregnant?"

"Oh, man." He blew out a long, exhausted breath. "I don't know, Janie. The timing isn't right. For any of us. I mean, think about you. How would you raise a baby in college? You'd be giving up everything you've always wanted. Your life would basically be, like, over. Everything would revolve around the kid. You don't want that right now."

I would be giving up everything. Except one, very important thing.

"And then there's me. My scholarship. Shoot, in three years I'll probably be going pro, or something. What would we do with a baby then? We'd have parties and autograph signings to attend. You can't just show up as a rookie with your baby in a stroller. They expect you to give your life over to them."

I almost laughed. "But, us? Do you think we'd stay together if I still had the baby?"

He leaned over and kissed my forehead. "Of course, babe. Is that what this is all about? I'm not going anywhere, if that's what you mean. You don't need a baby to keep me here."

I understood what he was saying, but his comment made me furious. As if it was my doing. As if I would do something so reckless in order to keep my boyfriend. He must have seen the flaring in my eyes.

"Not that you would do that—I know you wouldn't. We love each other, right? That's all that matters." Drew stepped to my side and put his hand against my back.

I suddenly felt homesick for the way things had been between us.

I ignored the fact we might be spied on as Drew and I stood in my front yard, holding onto each other as he stroked my hair and kissed me. If things had been different, I would have totally fallen for it. I would have felt a huge relief that we would still be together. That he still loved me, even after what he'd thought I'd done.

But I realized in that moment that loving each other didn't really matter at all. There was a bigger love at play. One I could never deny.

"Tell you what. I'm going to run into town and pick up something for us to eat. I'll be back and we can sit and talk. Like we used to. Before all . . . this." Drew motioned around my middle with a circular movement of his hands.

I watched him saunter back to his car, young and cocky, the boy I loved. He rolled his windows down, laid his arm nonchalantly against the door frame and put on a new pair of sunglasses. He looked so good in that moment. Young and beautiful. A striking contrast to the life ahead of me.

He pulled his shades down slightly, winked at me and called, "Later, babe."

"No, really. I need to get back to . . . um, my family."

"Okay then. Whatever," he said smiling. "I'll call you tomorrow."

His tires tore down the street and out of my life. Possibly for good.

Chapter Twenty-four

Purdy

I'd been calling over to Charlotte's all blasted day. If she missed this lunch, I would kill her.

I'd stepped out onto the porch, and watched as Janie and that loser boyfriend of hers made out in the front yard—in broad daylight. Tramp. Would she never learn? The second she walked through the front door, I dialed the number again. She was not getting off the hook.

"Oh, thank the good Lord. Janie! I've been calling over there all morning. Where have ya'll been?"

"Um . . . I don't know."

"Well. I was trying to reach your Mama about something and I finally got her on her cell just a minute ago. But, she forgot to tell you that she needed you to pick her up after our lunch today. We're dropping her car off at the shop, and she'll need a ride home."

"Why can't you just take her?"

"Because. I have a life. Can you be there or not?"

"Yeah. I'll be there. Fine." Janie said.

"Now, don't you go getting all snappy with me. This is for your mama. God knows she does enough for you."

"I'll do it."

I paused. "I guess that's not the first time those words have left your mouth."

Janie was dead silent.

Then I just couldn't help myself, you understand. I whispered, "Not that your situation surprised me any."

I could feel the heat rising in Janie over the phone.

"You know I heard that," Janie spat.

"Oh? Well I'm sorry then. I didn't mean it."

"You know, I think you enjoy being a troublemaker."

"Troublemaker? Troublemaker! Did you call me a troublemaker?"

"Well, you are . . ."

"Hold on. I need to write that down." I rifled through a drawer for a pencil and paper.

"No you don't—the judge can't do anything about me calling you names. Quit trying to get him involved, Purdy. It's embarrassing. He has more important things to do than listen to your ramblings."

"Ramblings!? How'd you spell that? R-A-M . . . oh shoot. Hold on."

I shuffled through the kitchen and opened the back screen door with a squeak. Tizzy stood there looking at me, but refusing to come in. I picked up the receiver again.

"What's wrong, Purdy?"

"Fickle cat. I can't keep her in the house when that boy is in the yard. Just be there, Janie. At 12:45. And, don't be late."

Everything was falling in place.

Chapter Twenty-five

Charlotte

Maimie convinced me to go to the ladies lunch anyway. I promised I would, but only if she came with me. I felt like a sacrificial offering, walking up to the volcano to be tossed haphazardly into the fire. There was no question I would be today's victim. Purdy was predictable about such things, if nothing else.

I dressed in my favorite white suit—before Memorial Day, which Purdy would despise—and made sure my makeup was flawless. I would go down looking impeccable, not like some downtrodden beggar I imagined Purdy wanted me to become. I hoped she would be anxious and impatient, unable to belabor the suspense. It all depended on how the conversation went. If no one offered something more tantalizing, Purdy would attack early to keep things interesting.

David hadn't come home the night before, though Janie had shared a text she'd gotten from him saying he was helping the Bryant's with their air conditioner and would be gone until later. I wondered where he'd slept, and when he would come home again. I hadn't realized how much I enjoyed our little conversations throughout the day, until he hadn't bothered to call me. I turned my ringer off before someone else called—someone else being Purdy, of course, aggravating me about where I was.

I showed up twenty minutes late, gave my keys to the valet, and marched forward into the clubhouse. As I approached the table, I noticed the seat open beside Purdy, with Maimie flanking the other side. Relief flooded my system and I smiled directly at Maimie who must have rushed to get there and claim that spot.

The other ladies nodded their greetings, and then eyed each other carefully. Purdy had obviously given hints as to something going on with me. Maimie seemed weary, but patted the seat beside her.

Purdy pretended to chat with Helen Matthews who was sitting directly across from her. I knew from years of Purdy's comments that she couldn't stand Helen. Still, she played her game, pretending to be deep in conversation, and ignored my approach.

I took my seat and placed a napkin in my lap as a waiter helped to slide my seat forward. I nodded to him, gave him my water glass, then took a sip before surveying the table. All eyes were on Purdy, with occasional glances toward me. The whole scene reeked of over-privileged obnoxiousness. I turned to Purdy and tried to catch her eye so we could hurry this along. When she pretended not to see me, I took the gracious route, and punched her full force in the arm.

"Ow! What in the world is wrong with you? You don't just . . . punch me." Purdy punched me back.

It hurt far more than I expected, and I punched her again. I winced as I turned to Maimie, who was completely amused, then back to Purdy as she punched me a second time. Purdy's eyes narrowed and a smug satisfaction spread over her face.

In one fluid motion that stunned even me, I picked up my water glass, took another sip, then spit it in Purdy's face. I was not going down without a fight.

Maimie exploded in laughter as the rest of the table sucked in a cautious breath.

Purdy picked up her own glass, took an even longer sip, turned straight to face me, then swallowed hard. She smiled at me through clenched teeth, and rolled her eyes as she turned her head back to the table, patting her face with her napkin.

"Well, as you can all see, Charlotte has gone completely off the deep end. The entire family is discussing having her committed," Purdy said. Some of the women around the table smiled at the joke, others seemed like they bought it.

"Of course, anyone forced to grow up with Purdy, is a medical miracle to have made it to forty without checking into an asylum." I smiled as I played along.

"Speaking of an asylum, did you hear about Jessica Hillman's son?" A newbie to the lunch group spoke up, her eyes lit with excitement over another's unfortunate demise.

I stared at Maimie, whose eyes darted down. I reached to squeeze her hand under the table. Why do I keep coming to these?

When lunch orders were taken, the usual fare was requested. Six of the twelve women ordered Cobb salad with dressing on the side, two ordered steamed vegetable plates, and two ordered chicken salad. It was the same every week, and I usually complied, not wanting to stand out or seem unladylike. When the waiter came to me, I hesitated.

"The same as last week, ma'am?" he offered.

"Um. No. Is there a pasta today?"

"Yes, ma'am. We've prepared a lovely pasta salad—"

"No. No salad, thank you. I mean pasta. Long noodles, messy red sauce, you know the kind?"

The waiter smiled, amused at the reaction of the other women who whispered as if I had given him my room key. "I'll have the chef work up something special for you."

"Thank you. So very much." I wiped my mouth neatly with my napkin and placed it gently in my lap.

"And for you?" He turned to Maimie.

Maimie winked at me and smiled. "I'll take the same. But, double the sauce."

The conversation idled as we waited for our food, and I became confused about why Purdy hadn't attacked. I'd noticed her looking at her watch more than once, and knew she was up to something beyond her normal deviousness.

Waiters began to float around the table as the ladies meals were presented under stainless covers. When the last plate was laid in place, the waiters lifted the lids in unison, revealing their choices. Everyone's eyes were on mine and Maimie's plates. We smiled at each other and tinked forks, as Purdy rolled her eyes.

"What are you, twelve?" Purdy spat under her breath. "What kind of woman gets spaghetti, in the middle of the day, at the country club for goodness' sake?"

"I like spaghetti," I mumbled, my mouth as full as I could possibly fill it. I slurped a long, renegade noodle, as it flipped from side to side, leaving a splatter of sauce on my white jacket.

"Good lord, do we need baby wipes here? You're behaving like a child. Stop it, immediately."

I turned to Maimie and rolled my eyes. Maimie filled her mouth with so much pasta that chunks of it fell onto her lap as she spoke. "This is the best spaghetti I've ever had. In like, my whole life. I mean, the best—" The last syllable caused Maimie to choke a little and a large chunk of tomato flew from her mouth, to the center of the table.

Ladies around the table clucked their teeth and glanced away, as if disgusted. That just made it all the more fun.

Maimie and I continued playing in our food, eating off each other's plates, and flinging noodles on each other's clothes. The table beside us had summoned the waiter to break it up, but he refused when he saw a Parker in the middle of the fray.

"That's it!" Purdy pushed back from the table, and stood, grabbing both mine and Maimie's forks in the process. Maimie locked eyes with Purdy, then dipped her hand into her bowl and pulled out a clump of noodles. She dangled them over her open mouth, and let them drop in. I choked on my water at the sight, and the two of us crumpled in laughter.

"You'd think you'd have better things to spend your time on, Charlotte. Your daughter's life is in ruin. You've destroyed our entire family. And, now, you align yourself with the town's latest reject."

The last words hit me like a brick. I pushed back from the table, stood to face Purdy, then pulled Maimie up beside me. "The only reject in this group, is you, Purdy. You, my sister, don't contain one ounce of decency. We are fully aware that you had every intention of filling our ears with the latest upset. Why else do you think these desperate-for-significance-wannabes even bother to show up each week? All they have are their pretenses. And, they're hoping that someone is more miserable than they are. That way, they can go home feeling better about their pathetic, self-centered lives."

I turned to the group and leaned in. "Well, I have news for you ladies. You will never win. Purdy is the queen. You will never leave here feeling any better than she wants you to. Because in the end, she can't go home until she has destroyed a little bit of each of you."

Purdy shook her head and rolled her eyes at me as if what I was saying was not to be trusted by the others.

"And, here's the clincher. You may go your entire life and not outdo the bad decisions I've made lately. So, let me lay them all out for you." Maimie grabbed me by the wrist as if to stop me, but I ignored the gesture. If anyone was going to spread rumors about me, I wanted it to come straight from the source. "My daughter Janie, who is still in college, and unmarried, got pregnant. She tried to hide it from me, but I overheard her talking about it to a friend. Her auspicious aunt over here convinced me there was only one way to save her future, and we forced her to have an abortion. Not only did I go along with her to the clinic, but I stayed in the waiting room while what they call a 'doctor' killed my first grandchild."

Maimie pulled harder on my arm, but I resisted again.

"So, have at it ladies, go tell your friends and family. Put it in the newspaper for all I care. That's what the Parker's have been up to lately. It's—how do you say it Purdy?—what we do. It's a sordid tale, but one I'm sure you will all enjoy retelling over and over again." When I was finished, I let out a long breath, wiped my mouth once more with my napkin, dropped it on the table, and picked up my purse to leave.

Turning to the door, I stumbled at the sight of Janie, dressed in her best sundress, hand to her mouth, tears streaming down her face. Before I could say a word, she rushed from the clubhouse and tore off in her car.

I turned toward Maimie, shocked and searching for help. Maimie' eyes teared up in response. I glanced around the rest of the table, but no eye would meet me—save Purdy's. She watched in pure amusement, tapped her watch, and resumed eating her meal.

Chapter Twenty-six

Janie

I knew just where I would go as my car sped through the long winding drive at the club. I missed Zee. Sometimes it seemed like he was the only one who saw me for me. The only person I could be around and not be judged. And, in some strange way, he was the only one who made me feel normal.

Mama's words reeled through my mind, torturing me. Is that what she did each week? Flaunted her family's secrets like tidbits in a one-up contest? I couldn't believe it. I hoped she was stranded there. That would show her.

In truth, I was the one who'd been shown.

I pulled through the streets, stopping in front of the children's home where Ms. Ellie worked, and Zee helped. It had been so long since I'd visited, and yet it still felt like home. A small cast iron sign with the words Grace House scrolled in auspicious lettering gave a different image from what I knew was inside. I wondered if most people even knew about this place.

Grace House seemed like any other home in the old rambling neighborhood as I pulled onto the long drive. A large, Georgia mansion on several acres of land. Pecan trees lined the edge of the gravel drive and I could see a circle of hydrangeas up ahead surrounding a small fountain. As I drove closer, I noticed a tousled haired boy sitting alone on the edge of the fountain. He was dropping in pieces of bread and talking to himself, or maybe the fish. He glanced up and waved, then jumped down to chase behind my car.

I got out and smiled at him as he walked slowly to inspect the rear window of my car, then ran off toward the back. Walking up the front steps, I thought about my own home. The oversized columns on my porch, the rows of perfect rocking chairs—though there were many more here. Here, wide planks lay side by side and hung off the edge of the porch creating a wide gathering space. Remains of people having sat recently were still on the table. It seemed so worn, so welcoming. I'd always wanted a house full of people, maybe brothers and sisters to play with, maybe cousins. Instead my porch was immaculate and cleaned each Tuesday. Mama would sweep it down, check for spider webs, and then realign the chairs in a perfect row. Not that they ever moved.

I pushed through the large mahogany door to reveal a beautiful carved staircase along one wall and an oversized desk and chair against the other. I expected to find children running and screaming, chasing each other up and down the halls—as Zee and I used to do—but it was incredibly quiet. Finding no other seats for guests, I sat down on the small desk chair, eliciting a loud squeak. It had been so many years since I'd been in this place. It seemed smaller now.

I wheeled around once in the seat, remembering how Zee and I pretended to be managing things when we were young. I wondered if we were the ones who had caused the squeak. On my second turn around, something brushed against my leg, sending me and the chair wheeling backwards on instinct.

The small fountain boy withdrew his hand from underneath the desk and giggled. If he was hiding from something, I didn't want to be the one to bust him. I peeked under the desk and made a funny face, sticking out my tongue. It felt like playing with Zee.

Instead of the laugh I expected, the boy's face went blank and he lowered his head to look at his feet. Had I hurt his feelings?

I had to make sure. "Hey, buddy. What's your name?" I whispered toward my feet.

No answer.

"Really? I've never in my whole life met someone named . . ." I intentionally left a blank. "It's nice to meet you . . . I'm Janie."

Giggles ensued and a small hand reached toward my own. My heart suddenly ached for him, though I knew nothing about him. He rubbed my forearm, testing, then slid his hand into mine. I pulled him out gently and sat him on my lap.

"Well, you are by far the cutest . . . I've ever met."

"Gabe," he whispered in a garbled voice.

"Oh, well that's much nicer. A very nice name, in fact." I smiled and winked at him. He beamed revealing a rectangular space where his top two teeth should've been.

"Well, now. I see you met the boss." Ms. Ellie rounded the corner from the other room and greeted me. As she smiled, her doughy face lit up, her eyes becoming two happy slits. She wiped her floured hands on a blue striped hand towel, readying to hug me. Gabe jumped off of my lap and rushed to Ellie, hugging her legs. She patted him on the rear, and he ran off toward a row of closed doors, stopping in front of the last one to glance back and give me a quick wave. I winked and he stopped himself before entering, attempting to wink back, but it came out more like a squishing of his entire face. Then he slipped inside the room.

"Drug dealer," Ms. Ellie commented, throwing me completely.

"Excuse me?"

"His mama. She was caught selling drugs. Actually, she was caught taking money for drugs. Gabe was distributing them. In a lunch box, from what I'm told."

"Oh." I didn't know how to respond.

"It's okay, honey. We all have stories as to how we got here. It doesn't mean our circumstances are a reflection of who we are."

I fit in perfectly.

"So, what are you doing here anyway? Did Zee trick you into coming or something? He'll be so excited to see you."

"No. I just . . ." In that moment, I realized I had no idea why I'd come. It seemed like the logical place to go, but now that I was there, I couldn't really say why. "Is, um, he here? I really need to see him."

Something in my eyes gave me away. I felt like I was doing a good job of hiding my emotions, but Ellie could see right through it.

"Oh. Are you sure, hon? I'm still available for that talk."

"Um, I know. Just, not right now, okay? Can I see him?"

Ellie put her arm around my shoulder and led me down the hall. I slid my fingers along the chair rail, skipping over what appeared to be classroom doors. Each had a small square window and I tried to peek in as we passed.

Just as I was about to pass in front of the door Gabe had entered, it flung open and he raced toward the front of the house again. The heavy front door creaked and slammed against the wall as a familiar car pulled around beside the fountain. I stepped onto the porch to see who it was.

"Is it up there, yet? Did you get one for me?" His tiny legs jumped up and down as he stared at the back of the car.

Gabby emerged from the driver's side, snapping her phone shut. "Well, I'm not sure I can remember . . . let's go see." She took his dirt stained hand and pulled him toward the back of her car. "Hmm . . . oh! There you are, the one on the end, with the baseball cap."

"That one?" He jumped as high as he could, unable to reach it.

Gabby straddled behind him to lift him high enough to see. He leaned against the trunk and traced the outline of the stick figure with his finger, lingering over the "U" shaped mouth.

He leaned his head on Gabby's shoulder, then slid down the side of her car and ran ahead of her into the house, jumping up and pumping his fist the entire way.

"It's hard to understand, isn't it?" Ellie asked, coming up beside me. "How their parents could walk away, I mean."

I shook my head.

"There really is no explanation. That's the worst part. Their parents can't see what they have. All they see are the problems. But, God can turn even that around."

I nodded, more aware than ever of the gift God had given me.

"Well now, Ms. Ellie, I had no idea you knew Janie," Gabby beamed as she came toward us carrying a box laden with small sets of clothes. "I've got a bunch for you today, Ellie, been collecting these for weeks."

My heart constricted wondering if I was about to be pulled into a conversation I had no intention of getting into. I searched Ellie's face, desperate to find a glimmer of something that would clue me in. The last thing I could bear was to discover disappointment in her eyes. I'd seen enough of that lately.

Ellie glanced quickly at my stomach, and her face softened as she came toward me with arms wide. She hugged me harder than I thought possible. When she was done, she pulled me back, looked me right in the eyes and said, "Janie, of course he told me. I wasn't sure what he meant at first. But, I figured it out. I've been hoping you would go ahead and tell me. I've been dying to tell you that even this, is from God," she said.

"It's okay," I said. "You don't need to say that, Ms. Ellie. This is my doing."

Ellie's faced changed as she took in my words. "Janie, no. No, Darlin'. You don't understand. I've spent most of my adulthood mothering these children. Some of them have come without parents and left that way into adulthood. But, each and every one of them—if you asked them the truth—would tell you they would give anything to be in a home with a family, regardless of what that looked like. Some of them get that, but most don't. Most parents walk away. Any parent who doesn't is just . . . well, incredible in my book."

My eyes burned as my jaw set tight against my rising feelings. A single tear trickled down my cheek and fell to the floor. Someone supporting what I'd done? My entire family was against me because of it. Behind me, a small child reached out to touch my arm, trying to comfort—Gabe. I imagined he knew a lot about losing a family and starting over.

Chapter Twenty-seven

Purdy

Daddy was flat out wrong about me. I was still in control. Running a three-ring-circus, I'll admit, but it was my circus show if nothing else. Everything was all out in the open now. We were the talk of the town, and I didn't even care—really, I didn't. No, really. I chose the role of helpless bystander, and made sure everyone understood that what had happened at that clinic was nothing I had anything to do with. I'd been forced, you see, by a sister who threatened to tell the world it was my doing if I didn't go along. So there.

A few days had passed and Thursday was upon us: tidy day.

I went to the closet and broke out the cleaning supplies and bucket, at nine A.M., like clockwork. As I reached over to gather them, a spot of something on my hand caught my attention. It wasn't quite dirt, or an age spot. But, it would not do. I was scheduled for a manicure tomorrow and I was not about to sit and listen to the manicurists wink and giggle in Korean about my aging hands.

I stood at the sink and washed. Once. Then, twice. It would not come off. I plundered through the cleaning bucket to find something stronger and pulled out a spray. I spritzed it on my hand and then scrubbed, but it remained still.

This would not do. I pulled out the bleach. I pulled out the steel wool. I poured a glass half full of water then added some bleach, dipped the steel wool in it and scrubbed again. Still, nothing. I grabbed the bottle of bleach and poured it straight onto my hand and scrubbed as hard as I possibly could. I was relentless with that stain. It was not going to outdo me.

The burning numbed after a few moments of scrubbing. I let the cool water run over my hand, the blood turning a pale pink in the bottom of my white porcelain apron sink. Then, I continued until my knuckles and the back of my hand were raw, ensuring victory was mine.

The sight of Mother at the sink returned to my memory. But, this was different. I was nothing like Mother.

Chapter Twenty-eight

Charlotte

I spent most of the afternoon driving up and down streets and through neighborhoods looking for Janie. I'd been to every friend's house I ever knew she had, and had even called Drew, but no one had seen her. At least that's what they told me. I went back to the house around dinner, hoping David was there. Maybe Janie had been in touch with him.

I pulled into the garage and was so happy to see his old truck there. The fan was still running under the engine and I wondered how long he'd been home. I had so many things I wanted to talk to him about, but I felt like I'd almost lost the privilege to do so.

I stepped through the mudroom and hung my keys on the hook by the door. I could hear David talking, and peeked in to find him on the phone. My heart rushed with hope, praying Janie was on the other end.

"Sure, tomorrow is fine. No, really. The late notice is fine. I can move a couple of things around with no problem. Especially since the CEO and VP will be there. I know their schedules are a lot more hectic than mine. Yes."

Is he job hunting?

"Yeah, that. The location thing may be a hard sell, but I'm up for discussion on it. Okay. Thanks so much, Bill. You're the best. Okay. See you then."

David hung up the phone and headed to our bedroom, not even noticing I'd come in. He sighed as he walked through the door, and I wondered if he was exhausted from a long night, or from dealing with me. He went straight to the bathroom and started the shower.

I entered the room quietly behind him. My heart caught as I found a larger suitcase on the bed, beside the smaller bag he'd packed only a day before. He had his clothes stacked by days, as he always did for trips, and I could see he would be gone for at least a week. He'd never left me for more than one night. I'd always accompanied him on trips longer than that. But, my suitcase was nowhere in sight. He had no plans for me to join him.

I began putting his things into his suitcase by habit, wishing I hadn't done his laundry. Maybe that would have made him stay at least one night. Instead, he'd be in and out in a couple of hours. Too easy.

His cell phone buzzed on the dresser and I felt a little guilty checking the caller ID. I didn't recognize the number, and the name didn't come up, just a long distance number and the words "Cell Phone GA."

Georgia? How far is he going to take this?

I was still standing over his things when he stepped into the room wearing a towel. He eyed me suspiciously, but said nothing as I casually stepped toward my jewelry box beside his things. I pretended to search for something, then slipped a miscellaneous ring on my finger as if I'd been looking for it all along.

"Going away again?" I asked cautiously.

"Yeah."

He wasn't going to make this easy. I opened his sock drawer and began pulling out pairs to match the outfits he'd prepared. I laid them by the suitcase, being careful not to touch him. He didn't respond.

"Can you at least tell me when you'll be back?"

He looked at me, then turned away going back into the bathroom, carrying a shirt and pants.

My shoulders slumped in defeat. Did I even deserve to know?

"Your phone was ringing while you were in the shower," I said.

He came back toward me and put his hand out for the phone. I placed it in his hand, lingering there. He eagerly checked the screen, trying to figure out what he'd missed. His eyebrows furrowed as if he was unclear.

"Hmm." He flipped it closed and returned to the bathroom.

"Who was that?" I hated myself for asking. "Has Janie called?"

"Bob. Givens. From Mayfield department store. In Atlanta." He ignored my last question.

The way he spoke made me wonder if he regretted each piece of information he fed me. He must have known the conclusion I would draw. Mayfield's had been after David for three years now. Stopping him at trade shows and sending him gift baskets over the holidays. I knew they had a deep appreciation of how he'd grown my family's company from a local clothing store to a regional chain in a matter of years. They made no secret of their attempts to woo him away. But, I never wanted to move to Atlanta. The traffic. I knew I'd hate it for that reason alone.

"So, that's it. You're going to do it."

"Do what?"

"Don't play games, David. We both know what's going on here."

"We do? I thought I was going to a business meeting." He feigned confusion, which infuriated me.

"At least you could tell me you were leaving."

"Okay. I'm leaving."

"This is not funny, David. This is our marriage. You can't just walk away from it. You can't just go off on some whim because someone asks you to. What about your family—" I stopped cold. Just because someone asks you to. Is that what I did with Purdy?

"You were saying?" David asked as he zipped his suitcase closed.

I forced myself not to cry. "At least tell me if you've heard from Janie. I know I don't deserve to know. And, I know she doesn't want to see me. But, I'm scared—worried about her." I paused and breathed deeply, trying to keep my composure. "Please, David."

He let out a long breath. "She's fine. I talked to her earlier. After your lunch. Great job with that, by the way."

"Well, I know you won't believe this, but it wasn't what it looked like. Purdy was just—"

"You know what? That's enough. Just that one word is enough for me to imagine what you and your friends were up to."

"They're not my friends."

"Really? Well, that's too bad, Charlotte. Because, apparently, they're all you have and you're exactly like them."

He grabbed his bag and headed to his car without looking back.

I sank to the bed, beside the smaller bag he'd left behind. As I lifted the handle to move it, David's Bible fell out. I touched its worn pages, longing to be close to him. Instead, I opened it to a place he had marked and read the words: If we confess our sins, he is faithful and just and will forgive . . .

Forgiveness. Was it possible?

* * *

I could barely speak when I called Maimie. Mostly broken sentences, some crying, and a lot of empty pauses. Maimie was at my door exactly twenty minutes after I hung up.

We sat at my kitchen table. The one where I'd lost control and had a complete meltdown. The one where Purdy and I had sat days later and plotted. The one where all of this had started that day I blurted Janie's secret to David. I cringed at the thought of who I'd become.

We didn't speak at first, I mostly cried.

"I think it might really be over. I can't believe it, Maimie. He's never left like this. Never without me." I wiped the last remaining mascara from my eyes and balled up the Kleenex, throwing it onto the table.

Maimie held my hand, bowed her head and seemed to be praying.

"How can you do that?" I asked, pulling another wad of Kleenex from the box.

"What? Pray?"

"No. Pray for me. How can you pray for someone like me, Maimie? Aren't you afraid that being around me is a bad idea? You know . . . the company you keep?"

Maimie smiled a kind smile. "We're all messy, Charlotte. You don't have the market cornered on that one."

"It sure feels like I do."

Maimie sighed as her head turned toward the window, "Not by a long shot."

From the noise in the backyard, I could tell Purdy was preparing to storm.

Chapter Twenty-nine

Janie

Zee caught up with me at Grace House. He was so happy to see me, he couldn't stop smiling and showing me off. Like I was something to be proud of. After the newness wore off, Zee and I headed to the back of the property to our old hiding place.

In the corner of the lot sat an overgrown row of firs. For many years, Ms. Ellie would plant the old Christmas trees, saying she couldn't bear to lay them by the road. The result was an open area nestled in their midst. We were so much older, I wondered if we would even fit. Or—more importantly—if something else lived there now. But Zee pulled me through as always, and I discovered it was still being used by him on a regular basis.

He couldn't contain his own smile and was holding his hands over his mouth in excitement. I wasn't sure I was ready to deal with him like this today.

"What's up, Zee?" I tried to ask with as much excitement as he had.

"Dad home," he said moving two fingers to the side to squeeze this tidbit out and then covering his mouth again.

"He came all this way to see you?" I asked knowing his dad surely had other reasons, but would never share that with him. It made me so angry the way he shunned Zee at every opportunity, then showed up at random points in his life. Like that somehow made him a father.

In a way, his daddy's selfishness was the reason Zee and I had gotten so close. No one could console Zee like me. And even though I didn't know anything of unrequited love from parents, I could see how it broke a piece of him each time his dad came and went. I hated Zee's father, and yet tried to make up for him at the same time.

"Look," he said holding out a blue baseball cap with a red and white "A" scrolled on the forehead. A signature in black marker was scribbled along the bill. He couldn't stop smiling.

"Atlanta Braves? That's awesome, Zee. Is that your name here?" I asked playfully, starting to enjoy the mental break.

He giggled and shook his head from side to side, then whispered "Brian McCann" and flashed the number one and six at me over and over again, his favorite player's number, I guessed.

I took the hat and held it up to the light coming through the fir branches so he could see me take a good, long look at his new treasure. He held his hands inches under mine, making sure I didn't drop it. I twisted to the left and the right, egging him on, and he followed. When I placed it on my head he got so confused with his hands that he lurched at me and gave me a huge hug instead. And for once, I held tight. He held on too, patting my back. Then, without really meaning too, I started crying.

It wasn't the first time he'd comforted me, but usually, I was able to break my problem down in simple terms to explain to him why I was sad. Nothing seemed simple about my situation now, and I had no intention of burdening him with something so horrible. He pulled away from me more than once, searching my face and waiting for an explanation. But I continued to pull him back to holding me, with no offer of a reason.

We sat encircled by the small grove for a full ten minutes while I cried and he rocked me back and forth, not understanding, but choosing to be with me just the same. As I slowed my ragged breaths and was able to stop heaving, I felt Zee ever-so-slightly lift the hat off of my head and place it on his own. It made me laugh and he managed to keep holding on.

We finally pulled apart and scooted so our hips touched side-by-side. I leaned my head on his shoulder as we peeked through the tree limbs to see the children in the yard beyond. It felt so normal. Like this was a happy place to spend a childhood.

"Zee?"

"Uh-huh?"

"Your dad's really lucky."

"Yeah," he said, fingering the rim of his hat.

"If I had a brother, I'd want him to be just like you."

Zee turned and tried to hide a smile that crept across his lips anyway. His eyes lit up and he tried to hide that as well. "Me too," he said, and crawled out from our hiding spot, holding his hand out to me to do the same.

I brushed myself off and patted down my hair. I started to turn to go back to my car when Zee grabbed my wrist and pulled me with him running recklessly through the backyard toward Grace House. He was like a wild animal, darting around bushes and trees, dragging me in his wake. I kept thinking I would cut loose at the first opportunity, but it never came.

When we reached the steps, a bell sounded.

He grabbed me around the shoulders and hugged me tightly, lifting my feet off the ground a little.

"Lub you, Janie," he said. "I still be your brother."

"Love you too, Zee," I said. "And, I'd really like that."

"Yeah," he said looking down at his feet. "But, I the big one, not you. You little sister, okay?"

"Of course I am. Big brothers take care of their little sisters. That's what you're best at."

He smiled a wide grin, and rushed into the house.

I couldn't wait for my child to meet their uncle Zee.

Chapter Thirty

Purdy

"Looky-here. Two peas-in-a-pod, I reckon." I pushed my way in between Charlotte and Maimie, and pulled up a chair. Noting the snotty pile of tissues on the table I said, "Do you people ever enjoy a drama free day?"

Charlotte pulled her shoulders back and lifted her chin to mimic Maimie's stance. Seriously? Like that was going to stop me.

"Well, help yourself to a seat why don't you?" Charlotte tried to appear nonchalant, refusing to acknowledge anything was wrong. She glared at me. "It's not like we were busy or anything."

"Oh, shut it, Charlotte. I'm so sick of your constant whining. Mother-of-the-year over here is bound to tire of it too, I imagine."

Charlotte's mouth fell open. "You're not going to do that here."

Maimie's head flipped toward me with a smile. Like she'd won or something. Had we even met?

"Fine. I'm here on business. I need to talk to you about David. Privately." I glared at Maimie, who didn't move.

"You stay, Maimie. Please. I'll get rid of the trash."

I pushed out a quick breath. "Trash. That's fresh. Almost funny, Char."

"Don't call me Char."

"Fine, butterfly," I examined my nails, ignoring the looks between Charlotte and Maimie.

"We're busy, Purdy. What exactly do you want?"

"Well now, I don't want to interrupt your little party of brag books. Or should I say, burning? Anyway, it's not what I want, Darlin'. It's Daddy. He's a bit miffed about your hubby heading off to the competition. Especially after all he's done to help you two out all these years."

"I don't know what you're talking about. David hasn't gone to the competition." Charlotte was convincing, but seemed unsure of her own words.

"Well, the word around the store is he's heading to Atlanta, to manage the new Meyer's chain." I surveyed the situation. Charlotte diverted her gaze. "Or . . . did you know?" I smiled slowly.

"Well, of course, Parker's Department Store is just a bevy of information." Maimie interrupted. "Did you know that just the other day I learned Judge Thomas used to be an ambulance chaser? Of course, that was after his stint as a prison guard."

My head snapped toward Maimie.

"Oh, I guess that one's actually true . . ." Maimie smiled at me, and then turned to wink at Charlotte. "Explains the loose standards in women, I reckon."

My jaw tightened.

Charlotte knew to jump in before it got any uglier. "Well, word around the store is wrong. As usual. He is in Atlanta, but it isn't for an interview. He's . . . visiting friends."

"Alone?" I leaned in, examining Charlotte's every move.

"Yes." Charlotte held her expression steady. "I couldn't leave Janie alone. You of all people should understand that."

I leaned back in my chair, my eyes not moving from Charlotte. Charlotte held her gaze, her face unchanged. Maimie's eyes danced, watching the Parker sisters prepare for battle this close up.

"Okay, fine." I spat. "Don't tell me." I pushed back from the table and snatched my purse from the center. "But when I leave, and you two start tearing me down, at least keep it interesting, will you?"

"Don't worry, Purdy. We have more amusing things to discuss than the happenings of a ragged old woman and her cat."

"I'm sure. You two could talk the paint off a barn." I pulled the door shut with as much force as I could muster and nearly stumbled down the steps because of it. Which reminded me. I had a score to settle.

Chapter Thirty-one

Charlotte

I woke early, startled by a noise outside. I tried to go back to sleep figuring it was probably a neighborhood cat—or Purdy's psychotic one—but struggled to find peace without David beside me. I lay there drifting in and out of early morning sleep as my mind worried about the day to come: Janie's last day before returning for exams.

Waking up had always been the worst part of my day, but never more so than today. I found myself at the mirror, half blind before inserting my contacts. I watched the blurred image as I brushed my teeth, wiggling my arm back and forth. It was an odd shape in the mirror, with no real beginning or end. A less fenced in version of myself.

I wrapped my hair in a loose bun, allowing myself a few hours of unkempt comfort without David there. I pulled on my white chenille robe and the pink satin slippers Janie had given me for Christmas and walked through the beams of moonlight trickling in through the windows.

I started straight for the kitchen, feeling my way through the darkness, but the sounds of heavy breathing of sleep drew me to the living room. David lay cramped on the leather sofa, still wearing his dress shirt and pants from his trip. His belt, shoes, and tie tangled into a mass on the floor. I picked up the items one by one, smoothing the belt and tie across my arm. I watched him for a moment, wondering if he had any idea of how much I loved him. He didn't deserve the way I'd been dismissing him. I didn't deserve him.

The belt slid from my forearm, the buckle clicking loudly against the glass topped coffee table. David awoke and turned to see me standing over him.

"Hey," he whispered in the groggy strain of an early morning voice.

"Hey," I whispered back, leaning down to smooth his hair.

His hand moved to push mine out of the way, and my heart fell.

"The bed is free, if you want to get some rest. I'm going out in the garden for the morning. I won't bother you."

He tried to stretch in the small span of cushions and groaned. He sat up holding his back.

"Do you want something for that? I can get you some Tylenol, or maybe Purdy has—"

David stared dead into my eyes.

"No. I guess that's not a good idea, is it?" I said barely above a whisper.

He laid his head in his hands and pushed his fingers through his peppered hair.

I started to leave, "Okay, then."

David caught my arm. "We need to talk, Charlotte."

Like a child awaiting punishment, my stomach sickened at what was to come. I searched his face for a hint, but found nothing.

"Janie left early this morning. I watched her do it. Zee interrupted her and they traipsed off somewhere together. Thank God he got in the way."

My hand drew to my heart.

"This has gone far enough. This is your family, Charlotte. Janie and I. We are your family. Not the Parkers. Us."

My mind raced to figure out where he was going with this. But, I kept drawing a blank. Fear and desperation filled me.

"David, I don't know how else to say it. You know how sorry I am about all of this. What can I do to make you believe that?"

"I don't really care about you being sorry, Charlotte. It's a little bigger than that, don't you think? This isn't something you can apologize for and charm everyone into forgiving you."

"I know . . . I wasn't trying to."

David eyed me suspiciously. "Your daughter ran away this morning, Charlotte. Does that even register with you? Do you care at all?"

My heart ached. Of course I did. They were everything to me. Why couldn't I make that clear?

"I don't know whether to trust you or not. I can't even believe I'm saying that. But that's how I really feel. Like, I barely know you anymore."

I tried to keep my composure, to keep from completely falling apart. "I barely know myself anymore," my voice caught. I turned once more to leave the room.

"So that's it?" David asked. "We're going to leave this—this gaping hole between us?" His voice sounded angry. "We're going to let Janie walk out and not even go after her?"

"No. I don't know what to do to fix this, David. I don't know how . . ."

"What? No Parker army lining up by rank behind you? Can't you make a decision on your own?"

"I . . . yes. I can make a decision. Without them."

"Then do it. For goodness' sake Charlotte, do something."
His face was torn in a way I didn't understand. Was he desperate
for me to choose him, or desperate for me to walk away?

"Do it, Charlotte. Make a decision for once in your life. Just
you. Alone. Make a choice."

I stared blankly, struck still by his growing rage. I'd never seen
David like this before.

"Make it. Now. Or . . . I will."

I still couldn't move.

From the kitchen, a desperate banging on the back door
startled us both.

Chapter Thirty-two

Janie

A Spring storm rushed through Riverton on my last night before I planned to leave. I wasn't sure how I would do all of it alone, but I was determined to at least start by staying at Ellie and Zee's for a few days. I'd already talked to my advisor at school and told him about the pregnancy. Funny how it didn't faze him at all. Apparently, they had a plan for such things and I would be allowed to take my exams at another date, as long as I did it within the next ninety days. I decided to leave early, before everyone woke, so there wouldn't be a fuss over me. I was so close to telling them the truth, a little emotional show like that might cause me to break.

Like a wayward vagabond, the storm pounded the fields and neighborhoods, searching for a place to rest. Mama fretted endlessly about the flowers she'd planted along the front walkway and whether or not they were rooted enough to withstand the storm. I spent most of my time staring at the television but unable to let my mind rest upon the shows we watched. Daddy still had not come home yet, even though he'd texted me that he would be there by bedtime.

As had become my normal schedule, I headed up to my room early in the evening, shortly after the dishes were cleared. Mama and I had eaten at the kitchen island, in silence. It was Daddy's favorite foods: fried pork chops, mashed potatoes, and okra. Mama had even gone to the trouble to make dessert—chocolate fudge cake with toasted pecans—which hadn't happened since she'd learned from Oprah that eating sugar after a certain time of day caused your rear-end to double in size, or implode or something. It was delicious, though I didn't compliment her. I couldn't bear to start a conversation.

Once in my room, I lay down on the bed but never got under the covers. I wanted my escape to be quiet and flawless. I knew Mama would hear me if I made too much fuss. I was a nervous wreck all night and barely slept even though the tapping of rain against my windows usually ensured a great night's sleep.

My mind raced with every possible future scenario: the pregnancy, the delivery, raising a child alone. I didn't know how I would do it without Mama and Daddy, not to mention Drew. I was scared.

At 5:45am the storm had died down and I couldn't stand it any longer. I snuck down the stairs with nothing but the clothes I was wearing. I'd packed everything in my car. I didn't leave a note. In some way, I wanted Mama to suffer, just as I had.

I kept to the edge of the hall, trying not to step on a loose board, lest Mama be alerted—a practice I'd pretty much perfected over the last years of dating Drew. As I passed by the living room, I noticed a lump on the couch and realized Daddy was sleeping there. I wondered how often that happened, and if it would continue.

I stepped into the kitchen on my way to the garage and froze, my heart suddenly racing. My breaths came rapidly as if I'd just run a marathon. I thought I might drop to the floor right there. God, please show me I'm doing the right thing.

Then, a bright light flickered across the kitchen wall in broken rays.

I peered through the window into the darkness. The light flickered again, this time closer to my head. I ducked down. As I eased my head above the sill, a man with a flashlight pointed under his chin stood directly before me. I dropped to the floor in a panic, as Daddy snorted and shifted in his sleep in the next room.

From the other side of the door I heard a muffled laugh. Zee?

I eased the door open slightly and slid through it to the back yard. A faint beam of light shown under the steps, highlighting Zee's eyes which danced from the excitement of scaring someone. I crawled halfway under the steps and put out my hand, hoping he would forfeit the one thing that would surely get noticed roaming in a neighborhood in the early morning.

"Zee, what are you doing over here this early?"

Ms. Ellie was the only one I had told what I was doing. I couldn't imagine why she would get him involved. He stared down at his hands as I tapped the flashlight, and then backed away from me, shaking his head no.

"Is your Mama up? Did you see her?" I glanced toward his house, nervous that the sun was starting to come up over the horizon.

"Tag! You it!" Zee whispered as he scrambled out from under the steps and ran wildly toward Purdy's house, flashing the light like a beacon.

"Zee, wait!" I let out a long sigh and followed him, hoping Purdy had slept in for a change. As I came to the edge of her yard, I could see Purdy on her porch holding her cat in one hand and doing something with a rake in the other.

I watched as Zee darted from side to side in a panic, being chased by the witch of his nightmares.

Chapter Thirty-three

Purdy

L ike a well set trap, that idiot boy fell into my hands.
I'd been waiting on him, knowing he would do as he always did, like clockwork. Tizzy had taken to early morning outings, and I soon discovered that boy was the reason why. Every morning he'd open up a can of tuna on his patio and sneak over to my house on his hands and knees. My mind stung with the thought of grass stains on corduroys and I wondered why on earth his mama didn't chain him in his room or something. I would never tolerate grass stains every single day.

That morning was no different at first, except for the drizzling rain. I saw him open his back door around 5:30am. He moved slowly and held the can up to the moonlight repeatedly as if he couldn't find the pull tab. Once opened, he sat the can on the patio and took the lid to the trash can, clear around the other side of his house. After what could have been enough time to clean my entire kitchen, it seemed, he returned to fetch the can. Then, he put on that stupid camouflage jacket of his, and pranced on over here. Well, crawled was more like it.

This time, I was waiting. Me and all twelve of my cookie sheets. Well, mine and a few I'd ended up with after the bake sale at the church this past Valentine's Day. What? Returning them was on my list of things to do.

I watched him creeping over here, and I stood to the side of the house, the cookie sheets lined in a long row. Once he stepped over the property line, he was fair game. He called to Tizzy, but I held her squirming and pushing to get away from me.

Then that fool got distracted by something and headed over to Charlotte's. I hoped he'd wake her. I continued to stand back, but kept a lookout for him, knowing he'd go back to his house at some point. Within a few minutes, I could see him running like a maniac across the lawns that separated mine and Charlotte's homes.

Just as he got to the edge of my property line, I threw Tizzy in his direction. She screeched and meowed as she became air bound, and with one long motion, I scraped the rake back and forth over the metal sheets. Apparently, that is the ticket to the world's most terrifying sound—at least that's what it looked like in Zee's bugged out eyes.

I could barely contain my laughter as he ran crooked and flailing back to his house. Served him right.

Chapter Thirty-four

Charlotte

David jumped to answer the door, while I stood behind him as a neighbor screamed in broken sentences about an accident. And Janie. And Zee. And a car.

Like a rag, wrung out and frayed, I fell to the floor.

David tried to move past me, but I gripped his leg, not letting him leave me behind. He pulled me to stand, linked his fingers in mine and ran as quickly as the two of us could manage through the light rain and darkness of morning. I could hear someone screaming. A familiar voice.

We cut through the bushes at Zee's house, holly leaves tearing fissures in my bare legs. As we drew near the street, I prayed. Desperate for my daughter to be okay. I searched the growing crowd for Janie. Thirty or more must have been gathered in a circle, looking at something. At someone. I couldn't see. All I could hear was the screaming. In a voice I couldn't understand.

Chapter Thirty-five

Janie

"Get David! Get David!"

I could hear Ms. Ellie screaming, but didn't fully understand why. I scanned the darkened street, trying to make sense of the scattered shapes forming a mismatched puzzle before me. In my hand was a flashlight—Zee's flashlight. But, I didn't think to turn it on. I gripped it so tightly, my fingers ached. I was confused and terrified all at once.

I called Zee's name, quietly. Wanting to scream it, but barely able to eek more than a small wisp of air through my lungs. My throat was closing. I couldn't breathe. Where was he? I needed to look for him. Make sure he made it home. The blackness crept in on me, crowding my thoughts and my vision.

Ms. Ellie's screams, terrifying and muffled, filled my ears. I could see others gathering around us, coming from their homes in the early morning light.

"Get your dad! Get David!" Ms. Ellie demanded, but my body refused to move, as did my mind.

I closed my eyes, trying to shut out the noise and chaos. Trying to replay the scene from the moments before. A flash of headlights. The screeching of tires. Something slamming into me. The horrific thump. My body thrust forward now and I vomited into the street.

A man. Someone I knew. Cupped my face. Asked me something about my dad. I stared at him, unable to speak. The tears and rain crowded my vision. He pulled a towel and wiped my mouth. He placed it in my hand and folded my fingers around it, then ran off in the same direction from which I'd come earlier.

My hand shook violently as I pried my fingers from the stem of the flashlight and searched for the switch. Blinded by the growing lights pointed in my direction, I was left confused, not understanding why I was where I was, or what they were looking at. Then I saw him.

The newspaper delivery man, Carl. Rushing between me and his car. Something was in front of his car. I was beside it. I got to my knees and pulled my body through the gravel and oil that seemed to be filling the street. Or, was that blood?

By the time I got to the front tire, I knew whose crumpled body lay along the side of the street. Horrified, I slowed, not wanting to see, but needing to be there. Carl typed frantically into his cell phone alerting the police. Someone beside me was talking to an ambulance.

Ms. Ellie checked Zee from head to toe, trying to stabilize his head with a bath towel someone had brought from their home. Blood seeped out of Zee's mouth and mingled with the light rain that continued to fall as I began crying at the sight of my precious friend. An emergency worker appeared, his years of study being put into practice in a nightmarish way. I pulled myself to my knees, my head pounding. I offered words of comfort to Zee, though my voice felt small and meaningless. God, no. Please not him. Please.

I heard ragged breaths and for a moment my heart soared, believing them to be Zee's. But, they were Ms. Ellie's desperate gasps for air as she lost control of the situation before her.

In the background sirens wailed and the yellow blinking of the dome light on the paper man's car flashed against the dark blue sky that was beginning to form the morning.

A scream erupted from the back of the crowd, causing it to part as if on cue. Mama rushed to my side, patting my face, desperate in her prodding. She looked frantically from face to face landing on Ms. Ellie's and then Zee.

"What happened?" Ms. Ellie begged of Mama even though she'd just arrived. "What? Someone—please."

No one spoke. She searched for answers as eyes averted and teared at once.

Neighbors continued to gather in a nearby lawn whispering and holding onto each other as if the horror before them was their own. The ambulance turned the corner and slowed as it spotted the scene. Carl rushed frantically around directing them and describing what had happened. Within moments, Zee was lifted onto a gurney and placed into a cavity of flashing lights and tubes.

Ms. Ellie heaved her body into the vehicle and sat at his side, still checking him frantically and murmuring things under her breath. She clung to Zee's limp arm, refusing to be comforted by the team of people on board. Siren's blared as they maneuvered around the growing mass of people in the street and sped off toward hope.

I remained in the center of the street, drenched and unable to move. The paramedics touched my head in the back and asked me questions I couldn't comprehend. Around us, the rest of the bystanders tucked in their robes and hunkered under their umbrellas turning to go home.

As they cleared, I saw her. Rollers in her hair, precious time and care taken to protect them with a plastic cap, green gardening clogs on her bare feet. Purdy moved in closer, watching. The scraping of rake tines dragged behind her.

Chapter Thirty-six

Charlotte

I headed toward the hospital while David took Janie home. I hoped Zee was out of surgery and secure in his room, for Janie's sake if nothing else. I walked through the main hospital entrance and stopped in front of the desk. An older woman, with gnarled hands and a protruding hearing device greeted me as I approached. On her shirt pocket was a small nametag with "volunteer" typed underneath.

"May I help you?" she shouted. I decided it was a good thing she worked away from the patients.

"Um, yes," I whispered, counteracting her volume. "Can you give me Zee Baker's room number?"

"The bakery? We don't have a bakery here, honey. Just a cafeteria, over that way," she yelled, flipping her hand repeatedly toward the long hall to the right. "It's no bakery, but they do bake the best muffins this side of Graceland."

I smiled politely. "No, ma'am. I said Zee. Maybe he's under Zedekiah? Zedekiah Baker?"

"Oh! I'm sorry, doll. I'm deaf as a door post and twice as dense. Let me see here . . ." She pecked on the keys in a slow, singular motion that made me want to grab the keyboard and do it for her. I leaned over the desk, crossing space the woman didn't seem to appreciate.

"Nope. No Zedekiah Baker here. He must've checked out or something. Sorry, love." The old woman smiled and a perfect set of white teeth stood in remarkable contrast to the rest of her time worn face. I thought of Flora's teeth in a glass by her bed.

I had a sudden urge to go home.

Chapter Thirty-seven

Janie

"Drink some soup, Janie," Daddy said. He sat on the edge of my bed red-eyed and pale. He tucked Granma Mimi's quilt around my legs and feet. "Come on, honey. The doctor said you need to eat something—here."

The scent of vegetables and beef filled my senses and I immediately realized I was famished. I pushed myself up on my pillows while Daddy held the soup to me, trying to help me drink. In the corner of the room, Mama coiled in a chair, holding a handful of ragged tissues.

For a moment, I didn't realize why she was there. Like the fog of a sickness, I wondered how long I'd been out and how I'd gotten into bed without realizing it. I took the soup, pondering the situation with each sip.

My eye caught on something in the corner of my room. A stuffed animal Zee had given me on my last birthday, even though I'd turned twenty. The thought of him flooded my mind.

"Daddy!" I screamed in desperation as he held me and rocked me back and forth.

"I know, baby, I know."

"Where is he?"

Mama came to the bedside and sat carefully on the edge as if she didn't belong. "He's at home, we think. I checked the hospital and then came back here."

"What are we doing here? We need to go. We need to be there with him."

Mama and Daddy stared at each other, each one's face clothed in worry.

"What?! We need to go! He's . . . he's the only brother I have, Mama. He needs me."

Mama nodded. "Okay, hon. Just try to clean up a bit."

I flinched at the thought of getting "ready". Did everything always need to look so perfect for her?

Daddy opened my closet and pulled out a pair of jeans and an old tee shirt. I pushed the quilt off of me and headed to the bathroom, pulling my clothes from his hand. My head ached with each pounding step. I stared at my face in the mirror, not finding the girl I knew. I smoothed my hair and rubbed my finger along the bottom edge of my lashes, a streak of sticky black attaching to it. My mouth hung at an awkward curve. A sadness I'd never seen on my own face. The result of a sheltered life—forever protected and kept secure in my little world. In one quick moment, that world imploded.

Attempting to shower, I realized small pieces of dirt and gravel still clung to my body. Maybe that's what Mama meant. I soon found myself sitting on the tub floor letting the warm water cover me as the salt of my tears blended with it into one sorrowful stream.

Chapter Thirty-eight

Charlotte

David refused to let Janie walk over, and so we drove around the block to get to Zee's. We pulled into the driveway, the last in a row of cars neatly tucked by twos. I wondered if the house would already be full of neighbors trying to do whatever they could. That was one thing about Riverton; people took care of each other.

David took Janie by the elbow as they walked past Zee's window. It was too hard for me to see anything inside. At the front door, I started to ring the bell, but was interrupted as the door flung open and a couple hugged each other throughout their walk to the car. I turned to watch them as the woman burst into tears after being seated. My stomach fell.

Janie opened the door without knocking and slipped inside. David and I followed and were quickly covered by friends and neighbors who stood around in quiet clusters, whispering. I could tell that every available chair in the entire house had been pulled into the living room. So many stood around in packs that no one took notice of us beyond the first glance when we entered. Janie eased down the hall, stuffed animal in hand, and I followed.

Some woman Janie apparently knew stood at Zee's door.

"Hey, Gabby," Janie whispered. The woman pulled her into a deep hug, and smiled slightly at me over her shoulder.

Zee's bedroom door was open, covered with overlapped colorings of animals taped randomly from top to bottom. It reminded me of our fridge the year Janie was in Kindergarten. I teared up at the thought of how quickly that time had passed us by. Ellie was almost lucky that way.

Janie edged gingerly toward Zee's bed where a lump of covers breathed evenly in and out. She just watched him. I was so glad he was okay. She started to move the covers back.

"Janie, don't," Gabby stood behind her, apparently there helping Ellie with Zee.

"Oh, I wasn't. I just wanted to check on him."

Gabby's hand moved quickly to her mouth and she tilted her head upwards as she began to cry.

"I'm so sorry about all of this. I don't really know what happened. It was so dark. I totally feel like it's my fault. But, he must be doing good—right? They already let him come home."

Gabby's tearful eyes met Janie's. "He's not here, hon."

My mind went blank. Did the woman at the hospital look up the wrong name?

"But, he is—right there." Janie nodded toward the covers. Then, I noticed a long strand of brown hair against the far side of the pillow. Janie spied it as well, looking frantically toward me.

Gabby reached out to touch Janie's face. "It's Ellie, Darlin'. She refused to leave his room. The doctor had to give her a sedative, she was hysterical, Janie." Gabby's eyes filled again and her body shook.

Janie pulled closer to hold her. Then stepped back, confused. "Where? Where is he, Gabby? He's not—"

"No, no. But, it's bad, hon. They had him transferred to Duke. He's unresponsive. A severe head injury. They don't know if—"Gabby stopped as Ellie's body twitched. The whole house seemed to sense her movement and sat still for one long moment. Gabby pulled Janie gently down the hall as far away from the crowd as possible. I followed.

"Janie, they're saying he doesn't have much of a chance. I'm so sorry," Gabby gasped and started sobbing.

I heard the words. I did. They ran through my brain like a flicker of lightning. Pinging the corners of my thoughts but not settling in them. "What? No—he's. He's okay, Gabby. Right? The old woman said so," I argued. But the woman hadn't said those things, and I knew it. I felt numb as I watched Janie fall.

Chapter Thirty-nine

Janie

A sudden rush of heat filled my body. I felt dizzy and nauseous all at once. My ears closed off from sound. A blackness crept in as my vision began to tunnel and I fell, slowly, slowly, to the ground.

* * *

I awoke in a hospital room, my head throbbing, and my vision slightly off. A television set played reruns of The Brady Bunch, with the volume low. I was alone. No one sat in the visitor's chair or stood beside my bed. It was nighttime, though I didn't know what day.

My door was cracked slightly and from the hall I could hear voices, my parent's and another's. A doctor?

I struggled to a seating position, accidently knocking over a tray placed too closely to my feet. The door opened and Mama and Daddy rushed in. The doctor fell in step behind them.

"Sweetheart," Daddy took my hand. "We thought you fell again. You have a real knack for that today. I don't know how you did it, but you managed to hit your head in the exact same spot as earlier. You were out cold. They insisted you stay the night, but we're staying with you, don't worry. ."

I reached behind my head to a large bandaged lump. My head ached, but not nearly as bad as earlier. I pushed my hair back and noticed the tube attached to my other hand, with some sort of fluid flowing between me and a bag handing on a hook. My heart fell as I remembered the day's events and started crying again.

"Oh, honey, don't. I mean, try not to, Janie. The doctor said you need to stay as calm as possible. Try not to get too upset. A head wound is very serious, honey. We need to do everything we can to keep you from increasing pressure on the wound."

"But . . . Zee."

"I know. I'm so sorry, Janie. We're all devastated. We want to get you better so we can go see him."

"I can't even remember what happened, Mama. That scares me."

"Well, maybe there's a reason for that. Maybe . . . God has a reason for that."

It had been so long since I'd heard Mama mention God outside of church, it felt odd. But, in a way, it filled me with relief.

"But, you don't understand. He's supposed to be okay."

"He is okay, Janie," Daddy said. "I mean, he was terribly hurt in the accident, but he's not in any kind of pain right now. No matter what happens, he's going to be okay." Daddy's voice trailed as he looked down, almost ashamed.

The thought sickened me. Why did everyone I know seem to shove children off as if they were expendable? "He was like a brother to me, Daddy. I loved him."

"I know. I'm sorry. It's just that I guess not everyone in life can look beyond the surface to find the wonder beneath. That's what makes you so beautiful, sweet girl."

I fell back onto my pillows, my hand resting on my stomach. The wonder beneath. Was my baby okay?

Chapter Forty

Charlotte

We sat in an unfamiliar pew, in a church I'd always believed to be fanatical. Janie sat between me and David, barely holding onto both of our hands and staring blankly at a band getting ready to play. A band. In church.

Ellie had asked us to come. I turned to watch the stream of supporters from all over the county file in to pray for one boy's life. From the back of the crowd, a red feathered hat flitted from side to side, looking for someone, paying no respect to the solemn atmosphere or the reason we were here. One huff from the woman's mouth alerted me to the fact that it was my sister. Purdy's gaze narrowed as she saw me and I wondered what in the world she was upset with me for. Not to mention, why on earth she was even here—this wasn't a place to be "seen".

I turned to face forward, dreading the service now more than ever. I leaned my head atop Janie's and kissed her hair, closing my eyes to draw in the scent of my precious daughter. A figure pushed in beside me, I sighed, and then turned to find Maimie

Cramer sliding in. I smiled and couldn't help but laugh a little. I leaned into her, thankful for such a good friend.

Moments later, Purdy arrived at the side of the pew. She hovered over me with a scowl on her face, tapping her foot as if Maimie had taken her spot. David turned to his right, noting the packed pew, then shrugged his shoulders at her with a smirk. Purdy tore away from us as loudly as was possible on a purple velour carpet and pranced across the front of the church to find a spot in the darkened alcove of a side door.

Soon, every seat in the mega church was filled, with additional people lining the walls on each side. I wondered if something like that offered comfort to a mother in Ellie's situation, or if comfort ever came. Zee had not improved from the day of the accident. He held steady, but did not show signs of being able to hold his own. His brain activity was low—something the doctors kept a constant watch on.

A quiet song erupted from the worship leader in front who sat on a single stool, playing his guitar. The song seemed too happy for the moment. Too playful for the events that had just shaped our lives.

Ellie came in from the front followed by a string of people whom I assumed were family members. She was dressed in white and cried quietly, but smiled a broken smile to the crowd before her. She took her seat in the right front pew as the others filled in around her. If Zee's father was there, I wouldn't have been able to pick him out.

The service began simply. A series of photos from Zee's life flashed on a large screen at the altar. Baby pictures. School pictures. Family reunions. Christmases. Halloweens. His life in a carousel. A tattered picture of him and Janie at the age of four splashing each other in a plastic swimming pool flashed. I caught my breath and Janie moaned with grief. Ellie turned toward us and smiled a sad smile. I pulled Janie into me, as did David, creating a cocoon around the child we couldn't comfort.

Children from the home Zee and Ellie managed sat on a side pew slumped and huddled together. Ms. Ellie glanced upward, tears streaming down the sides of her face. Beside her, the woman, Gabby, leaned into her.

As the service labored on, I couldn't focus on the words of the pastor. I couldn't rid my mind of the thought that it could have been Janie. And, though Janie had little memory of the accident, I learned from the police that she had been the target, until Zee rushed from the side of the street he'd already crossed, to push her out of the way. Janie would never forgive herself if she knew. I would never forgive myself for driving my daughter to leave.

Lord, please forgive me. I've been so careless with my daughter. I know I'm not worthy of forgiveness after what I've done, but please . . . give me another chance. Help me to do something good for a change. And, Lord, Zee. Please do something. Don't let it happen like this.

The pastor paused, raised both arms at once, and the audience rose. He began again. "No matter how they come into our lives, children remain the most precious gifts of our hearts. Whether we are blessed with our own children, grandchildren, or are given the extraordinary honor of watching over another's child, they are a gift to enjoy. A gift to be cherished. A gift to celebrate. Zedekiah is such a gift, Lord. And today we reach towards healing. Hear our prayers, Father. Take the power you've given us to heal, and place it over him." The pastor reached his hand out over the crowd as a few, at first, then hundreds of people reached back towards him in the same motion.

"Father, we don't know why this has happened. But, we know that you are in it. And so, we will consider even this, as a gift in our lives. Because we know that in your works, nothing is wasted. And we praise you for that. James 1:17 says, 'Every good and perfect gift is from above, coming down from the Father of the heavenly lights, who does not change like shifting shadows.'"

I sat frozen in my chair, mesmerized by his words. Every perfect gift. Whether our own children or our grandchildren. Never changing. I closed my eyes and prayed for Zee, reaching my hand towards the altar in hopes that it might make a difference somehow. When I reopened them, I turned toward Purdy, who rolled her eyes and shifted in the shadows.

Chapter Forty-one

Janie

It had been several days, maybe a week or more, since the morning Zee had been hit. The morning I almost lost the only person in my life to ever truly love me unconditionally. I hadn't realized what an impact it would make, until he was no longer there to turn to. I had hoped that the prayer service would result in a miracle, but as of yet, there was no miracle to be seen. Still, he was steadily hanging on, and now that I had improved, I was cleared to go see him that night after some tests he was to undergo, I couldn't wait.

The accident changed everything for me. I knew I had to face my family and tell them the truth. And then I would move on—with or without them. I was pretty sure it would be without them. They wouldn't show mercy to me. And, as much as I wanted to beg for it, I wouldn't allow myself the opportunity.

Shortly after lunch, I took a walk around the neighborhood to clear my ever-crowding thoughts. I strolled along the side walk, allowing myself the time to reminisce my childhood. Taking in the familiar scents of the places I'd grown up around, I studied each home and considered the families represented inside. Were they as happy as they seemed to be? I'd babysat for all of the young families, run errands for Mama's friends, and even brought newspapers and mail in from the street to the elderly neighbors as Mama requested me. I thought of Grace House and the children there. How each of them would love to be given the opportunities I'd been given.

I was twelve weeks pregnant. My baby was the size of a strawberry, could move its arms and legs, and had the ability to suck its thumb. Each day my child grew inside of me, my heart grew to love it more. I knew without a doubt the baby was more important than what my family would decide.

I built up the nerve to approach the house and turned at the black and brown engraved street sign that signaled my street. I closed my eyes, took one last breath, and stepped toward my future.

Thoughts of Drew suddenly flooded my mind. I knew telling my parents the truth would lead me into something else I didn't want to do: tell Drew the truth. But, I'd fretted over my decisions for long enough.

I didn't know what made me do it. Whether it was the calming effect of the canopy of leaves from the hundred year old oaks that lined the street, or the hope that the light filtering through them offered, but I dialed his number. Whether Drew realized it or not, we were forever bound. And he deserved to—needed to—know that.

"Drew's cell," a pixie-like voice giggled. I could hear Drew in the background asking her to stop and laughing at her attempts to keep the phone away. Fire rushed through me.

"Let me speak to him, now," I pushed through gritted teeth.

"Um. No. He's . . . not available right now. Can I help you?"

"I'm pretty sure you don't want to get to know me that well. Give him the phone. Now."

Pixie-girl laughed. "Un-uh. He's busy. With me. He'll call you later." Then, she hung up.

The mental image of me strangling a skinny waif flashed through my mind. I dialed the number again. No answer. I dialed again. A pick-up-hang-up. Then, not really understanding what had come over me—let's say hormones—I dialed his parent's home.

"Mrs. Jacobs? Hi, this is Janie."

"Oh hi, sweetheart. Drew's not—"

"Yes, ma'am. I know. I'm having a hard time getting him on his cell phone too. Can you get him to call me as soon as possible? We need to discuss his baby. You know, the one I'm pregnant with right now? Thanks." Then, I hung up.

Drew returned my call without delay.

"Are you insane?" Drew yelled through the receiver. "Why would you say that to my mom, Janie? She came out to the front yard and dragged me in like a child. She is furious. She thinks you're serious."

"I am, Drew."

"No. I know," he lowered his voice to a whisper, "I mean, I know, but you're not anymore."

"Who answered your cell?"

"That? Oh that was Julianne. A friend from high school. She stopped by to drop off my jacket."

I didn't speak. That little tramp is fast.

"What? Are you mad about that? Come on . . ."

"Drew. I need you to come over here. Right now. I'm giving you thirty minutes, then I'm calling your dad at the church."

Twenty-two minutes later, his car rounded the curve.

Drew lumbered toward me in a pair of flip flops and jeans that were fraying at the bottom and his Franklin High Soccer tee. His hands crossed his chest and a scowl grew on his face. I wondered how long someone could get away with heralding their high school accomplishments after graduation.

"Janie, my mom is peeved. Why would you do that to me?"

"I needed to talk."

He stared at me incredulously.

"Seriously. We need to talk. And, I don't appreciate being dodged by Julianne." I said her name like a mocking game, and then felt childish and ridiculous for acting that way.

"Well. Get it out so I can get back and calm my mom down."

I watched him, standing there so full of anger, a nervous wreck over what his parents were going to do to him, and didn't want it to be like that. I didn't want him to hate me for what I'd done, but more than that, I didn't want him to find out about his child in anger. I was barely a parent and had already put my child in a precarious situation by playing games.

"I . . . um. I . . ."

"What? Man, you are really making me mad. This better be important. I mean it, Janie."

"It is. Very important. I . . . um . . . want to break up." The unexpected words fell out of my mouth, shocking even me.

"Are you kidding me?" he asked. "You're playing games with me, and now this? Fine! Done!" He yelled and stomped toward his car. Before he was even off of my curb, he was pushing digits on his cell phone. Julianne's, I was sure.

* * *

I walked straight through the house, out the back door and sat on the steps. Around me the trees were beginning to bud with new life. The scent of fresh grass and flowers perfumed the air. Clouds puffed across the blue sky creating a picturesque covering to a horrible day. A back screen door shut in the distance and as if by habit, I looked across the yards for Zee.

A pain gripped me and I wanted so badly to see him running across our yards. To tell him I loved him. To tell him he was the only brother I'd ever wanted. Instead, I crawled underneath the steps and sat in the soft, worn dirt where we'd talked so many times before. In the corner of the space, something caught my eye.

Bracey, muddied and wet, lay in the few sprigs of grass that managed to sprout under such a sunlight destitute place. A little napkin was tucked in quarters and placed under her head. I rubbed the doll's face, longing to remember what Zee looked like the last time I'd seen him holding her. I picked Bracey up gingerly, as a wadded pile of toilet paper fell from under her dress.

Had Zee been pretending Bracey was pregnant? The thought broke my heart. Like so many things in Zee's life, he always stood as a witness to other's lives, not fully understanding, not fully participating. Through the years, I'd watched as others pushed him to the side, or made fun of him behind his back—all the while, he remained unaware. I wondered if a baby was something he longed for himself one day.

I crossed my arms on my knees and buried my head in them, wanting to remember my friend. "You be okay. It'll quit hurting when the pain goes away." The words he'd used so many times under these very steps pulled at my heart. He truly loved me. No matter how imperfect, how abnormal, how ridiculous my life became.

I wondered how on earth Ms. Ellie would survive if she lost him. I crawled out from under the steps and brushed myself off. I took Bracey to the faucet and tried to clean her up as much as possible after all those years. But, as the dirt and dust blended instead of giving way, I thought of how imperfections were sometimes the most beautiful part. I patted Bracey off, and headed toward Zee's house.

I entered through the back door as always and found Ms. Ellie at her stove, stirring a steaming pot that smelled of brown sugar and cinnamon. A few people I remembered from the prayer service sat at the kitchen table talking with her. Zee's chair was empty. I closed the door behind me quietly, though everyone was fully alert in the house.

"Ms. Ellie?"

She turned, the dark circles under her eyes revealing her recent days. She smiled warmly at me and outstretched one arm. I walked to her and nestled in beside her. We stood there for a moment, not speaking, just holding on.

"I wanted to give you something, maybe take it to Zee," I said quietly. "It's a doll my Grandma made me when I was little. But, I never really played with it much. It's Zee's favorite. I thought he might like to have it."

Ms. Ellie flipped the switch on the stove and moved the pot to a back burner. She opened her hand to hold Bracey and took her lovingly into the crook of her arm, like a baby. "Oh, I know Bracey." Ms. Ellie grinned.

"You do?"

"Oh yes. She's been a guest in this house many, many times."

"She has?" I smiled at the thought and searched my mind to think of a time that I knew of that Zee kept Bracey overnight. I couldn't recall a one.

"You're right about one thing, Janie. It's his favorite. Or, at least the one thing he continues to bring home. I' always make him take her home in the morning, but yes, she's spent many a night in this house."

I smiled. I loved the idea of Zee caring that much for Bracey.

"Well then, it's settled. This is where she belongs." Warmth flooded my body.

"Oh, I know exactly where she belongs," Ms. Ellie said and smiled an old smile, like the ones she'd smiled in happier times.

A pain struck me in my side and I bent into it, letting out a cry.

"Are you okay, hon?"

I held my waist and tried to stand, but the cramp grew worse and I found myself sinking to the floor.

"Janie, here—" Ms. Ellie came to my side and grabbed my elbow. She tried to lift me into a kitchen chair, but the strength was gone from my legs.

Ms. Ellie flumped to the floor beside me, rubbing my back and looking me over. She searched my face for answers, evidently not finding what she wanted. She leaned over, trying to push herself up off of the floor, and stopped on her hands and knees. "Oh . . . Janie," Ms. Ellie whispered in a shaky voice.

Droplets of blood dotted the floor.

Chapter Forty-two

Purdy

I'd laid low during that boy's crazy prayer vigil and beyond. I mean, I went and all. I had to. Everyone in town was there and I knew everyone knew how I felt about him. I wasn't about to take the fault for that disaster. I hated it happened, though. And, in the last weeks, I think Tizzy missed him.

I stopped over at Charlotte's without calling first—rude, I know. But, I didn't care. I was finally beginning to understand what was going on with her, and I would not have it.

I entered through the kitchen to find her sitting at the table, snapping peas.

"So that's it, then? You're a holy roller? That's why you're acting so high and mighty lately? You've found your calling?"

Charlotte sighed, tossing her harvest back into the box.

"So tell me, Char. What is it? Destitute women? Drug addicts? Who in the world has God put you in charge of—bless their hearts."

"Leave it alone, Purdy. I mean it."

"See. I told Flora. I knew if I sat around here long enough, I'd figure out what kind of ridiculous nonsense you were up to. I was thinking you and David were going to high tail it out of town and leave the family business hanging. But, turns out, you're a bonafide Bible thumper. Before my very eyes, a real live Fundie."

Charlotte lowered her eyes.

My phone rang at an obnoxious volume, playing "Devil with a Blue Dress." Charlotte choked a laugh.

"What?" I snapped. "Blue's my favorite color."

Charlotte nodded, her hand pulling to her heart.

"Good gravy. Can't you handle anything without me? Fine." I hit a button on the phone, then another, then another. "What is with all these buttons? Can't they just make one that says on/off?"

Charlotte leaned in and hit the off key, clearly marked.

"Those pathetic newbies at the Junior League. Some kind of raffle ticket debacle. I swear, I don't know how this town managed before I took over." I grabbed my things and trotted out the front door, onto the porch.

Charlotte followed behind me and watched as I rushed down the steps and toward my house. Midway down the sidewalk, my silver heel sank into a dollop of red clay oozing between the brick walkway. Glory be.

As I yanked and cussed, I heard Charlotte quietly shut her door behind me. Don't think for a minute I didn't see her through the sidelight window laughing at me squawking madder than a wet hen.

Chapter Forty-three

Charlotte

At my insistence that he needed to sleep in a bed rather than the couch, David had taken to doing so in the upstairs guest room—not what I'd meant. I'd hoped the recent upset with Janie had drawn us closer, but I could see now that it had been temporary. I climbed the stairs with cleaning tools in hand intent on filling my day with cleaning out closets and going through old clothes—two things I could never get help with. David had taken my car to the shop for an oil change, so shopping or anything else fun was out.

I started in Janie's room, surprised to find it was fairly in order. Janie had been making her own bed for years, though she left it a little disheveled for my taste. I smoothed out the quilt and fluffed the pillows, turning them so the sagging bottoms were no longer noticeable. I straightened the edges of the sheets and leaned down to tuck them under the mattress. A small slip of paper fluttered to the floor.

My heart tore as I read the talking points my daughter had carefully listed. I wondered when Janie had originally planned to tell us, and if my reaction would have been any different than the one I'd become so ashamed of. I tucked it back in, and sank to the floor, regretting so much of the last weeks. I buried my head in my hands.

A floorboard creaked in the hall and I panicked knowing Janie would think I'd been snooping. I shoved my things into the cleaning bucket and jumped to my feet. At the peak of my rise, David came around the door and smacked directly into me, knocking me into the bedside table. A bottle of water and an old princess phone hit the floor.

"Charlotte! I'm so sorry. Are you okay?" David laughed but seemed genuinely concerned. He grabbed the paper towels and wiped up the water, taking time to see if it had gotten on me.

"Yeah . . . but next time, just trip me coming down the stairs okay? It'll be more effective."

"Aw, come on now. You know that wasn't on purpose."

"No, I know. I'm on your side, trying to help rid the house of . . . troublemakers."

He chuckled. "What? Your sister is banned?"

"I wish," I smiled.

David smiled in return. He glanced around Janie's room, leaning to touch a soccer trophy from years ago. His face turned serious. "We can't keep putting this off, you know. We need to talk, Charlotte."

"I know." My heart sank, unable to bear my own thoughts of what that meant.

"I want this to work, Charlotte. I don't like all this tension between us. But, I feel like I can't trust you anymore. Like, the very second I relax the Parkers are going to sneak behind me and carry out whatever outrageous plan they've concocted for their entertainment, without me knowing about it. It's like I can't maintain a handle on my own family. Like I'm one of their children and have to play to their whims."

I nodded.

"But, I'm not. And, I won't. I need you to understand that. I have to come first here, Charlotte. Me and Janie. You have to agree to that, or we can't move forward."

"I know . . ." My mind filled with images of the Parker women. I was like a toy to them, reacting to their every whim. The thought angered me, but mostly saddened me. Did they care about me at all?

"You're right, David. I can see that now. And, I'm trying. I really am. I don't want to be a part of their mess anymore. I just want you. And our family. You're all I have."

David took my hand in his and kissed me. I leaned into him as a passion from my past grew.

A persistent buzzing erupted from the cleaning bucket. We parted and David reached inside to find my phone, with Purdy's name flashing on the backlit screen. He eyed me carefully.

I grabbed the phone and he huffed. "What? I can't answer her calls now? "

He threw his hands in the air.

"But, you don't understand, David. She never calls my cell. It might be an emergency." I glanced at the phone dangling off the hook on Janie's floor. "Really."

"Do whatever you want," he puffed. He lifted himself off of the floor and slammed the door behind him.

I closed my eyes, the buzzing pressing me. "What?" I screamed into the phone as I accepted the call.

"Charlotte, I've been calling the house. It's Janie. Ellie called. She's taking her to the hospital."

Panic rose in my chest. "David!" I screamed with all the might of a mother gripped in the fear of the unknown.

Chapter Forty-four

Janie

With a towel stuffed between my legs, I crawled into the back seat of Ellie's car, frantic and confused. I lay down, clutching my stomach and curling into a ball. I could smell the blood. I stared at the ceiling, tilting my head toward the window. Flashes of tree limbs, intermittent stretches of light, and clouds pulled us along the street. They blurred as Ms. Ellie sped faster.

I could hear Ms. Ellie on the phone in a low voice.

God, please. Not now. Not after all this. Please don't let me lose my baby.

"Janie? Stay with me, hon. We'll be there in five minutes."

Chapter Forty-five

Purdy

Charlotte, David, and I rushed to the car. David slammed the Mercedes in reverse and screeched out of the driveway. Charlotte leaned her head against the window as David flipped off the radio and took her hand. "Pray, Charlotte."

Oh, good gravy.

"Um. Okay," she said uneasily. For my benefit, I'm sure. "Lord, please," was all Charlotte managed to squeak out.

That was it? I mean, really, they were trying to one-up me with God, and that's all they had? For pity's sake.

We arrived at the emergency entry moments after Ellie and Janie.

"May I help you?" A clerk asked.

"Yes, our daughter was just brought in. She's . . . bleeding. We need to get to her." David searched the area behind the front desk, annoying the clerk further.

The clerk straightened up in her chair. "Name?"

"Janie. Janie Johnston."

"Charlotte! David!" Ellie stood at the entrance to the triage, holding the door cracked.

They fled from the station and into the ER to meet Ellie. I rushed quickly behind, not wanting to be left in that nasty-diseased-filled-waiting-room.

"Ellie, what in the world?" Charlotte hugged her desperately, and took her hand. "Please, where is she?"

"She's in there. But, I need to tell you something first. I mean, I can't tell you, of course, but she needs to tell you and you need to keep an—"

"Mama?" Janie called through a drawn curtain.

"Yes, baby." Charlotte parted the curtains and slipped through. Janie sat angled in the bed, the sheets drawn in a tent fashion, bending at her knees. I stayed hidden from view.

"Mama. The doctor's coming any second. But, I need to tell you something first."

"Janie, what happened? Did you fall? Did something hit you? What?"

David slipped in behind Charlotte, his face full of concern. "Janie. Thank God you're okay. We got here as fast as we could, Darlin'. What happened?"

"I'm okay. I mean, I think I am. Listen, I need to tell you something."

"Are you bleeding? Is your head hurting again? Oh my gosh, David, what if she has another head injury in the same spot? You know what the doctor said about being careful. That another injury before it healed could—"

"Mama! Daddy! Stop. I need to tell you something. Before the—"

The curtain parted with no warning and a young PA in a doctor's coat entered, exposing my hiding place.

"What is she doing here?" Janie spit between clenched teeth. "What is this? Another plot? Get out! All of you! Get out of here, now!"

David slipped his arm around Charlotte's waist and forcibly pulled her through the curtain as she struggled to get to Janie and a plump nurse entered the room. The nurse smiled politely at us as we left and began to pull the curtains once more. As she did so, I watched Janie place her feet in stirrups and inch forward to the end of the table. My stomach plummeted. How could I have missed this?

Chapter Forty-six

Charlotte

David, Ellie, and I sat in a row of wooden chairs covered with navy blue cushions. Janie was in the maternity ward for some reason and it broke my heart that she might see the beautiful little babies in the nursery, or the pink and blue decorations that celebrated each door. The layout to the waiting room reminded me of the clinic that day. Here, I could understand why you'd want to face each other and talk about the new baby in your life. Here, you wouldn't be bothered by the uncomfortable chairs and lack of ambience. Nothing could steal your joy when a new baby came into your life. I wondered why I hadn't seen my grandchild that way.

I was glad Purdy's nosey self had been too busy to notice where the nurse had directed us. Ellie fretted in her chair, checking and rechecking the clock. I could tell she knew something.

God, can you hear me? I feel like I'm talking to air. I want to know you're there. Watching. Please, show me that much. I need you to be with her. Please.

David stepped away to find a cup of coffee somewhere in the building and I jumped at my one chance.

"Ellie, please," I begged. "Mother-to-mother. Can't you tell me?"

Ellie's brows furrowed and she shook her head. "It's not my place, Charlotte. Truly. You need to talk to Janie about what is going on with her."

"Well anyone in plain sight could tell you what is going on with her, Charlotte." Purdy clucked her teeth and I cringed that we'd been found.

"How did you get back here, Purdy? You know Janie doesn't want to see you."

"What? The neighbor can come back here, but your own flesh and blood can't? She's my niece, Charlotte. Plus, I have connections."

I sighed and rolled my eyes. Connections. I longed for obscurity.

"So did you solve the mystery, or must I constantly inform you gaggle of airheads?"

I looked at Purdy with reluctance. "I think I know. But, I wasn't able to talk to Janie thanks to you. You really need to go."

"Well, do you know, or don't you know? Should I just spill it, or do you want to prolong this all evening?"

"I know. She's pregnant. Again. Go ahead and humiliate me for not being a proper watchdog, Purdy."

"She's . . . what?! My gracious, Charlotte. You really are a piece of work. Not only diarrhea of the mouth, but constipation of the brain, I'd say." Purdy laughed and shook her head, mocking me. "She's like a hussy in heat, that one. You really have your hands full."

I leapt from my chair and smacked Purdy full across the cheek, leaving a four-fingered mark. Purdy's mouth fell and her hand flew back, ready for a cat fight.

"Whoa, whoa." David rushed over, spilling his coffee down the hall. "Easy, killer. Step back, now." He pulled me to the side and bared his teeth at Purdy, then snickered at the sight of us.

"What's so funny? Your lunatic wife tried to kill me." Purdy snapped.

"Yeah, well, sometimes I'm too quick on my feet. Next time I'll walk slower."

Purdy pushed out a loud breath and growled.

I rubbed my hands, nursing the stinging sensation that remained.

The double doors of the main floor opened and the PA came through, pulling off his mask and smiling at the ragged bunch before him. David, Ellie, and I rushed to greet him.

He held his hands out to slow us. "She's fine. She's resting now. We need to keep her overnight, to keep an eye on things. You can see her now if you want, but visiting hours end soon."

"Can you please tell us, can someone please tell us what exactly is going on with her?" I pled.

"As much as I'd love to, Mrs. Johnston, I can't. I know you're her parents, but she's an adult. Only she can. But, I think she's looking to see all of you." He glanced behind us to Purdy. "Well, most of you. She's asked that her aunt be escorted off the floor. If you don't leave ma'am, I'll be forced to call security."

With that, Purdy twirled around in a huff and stomped out of the maternity ward. As she passed the window of babies, I swear they all started crying at once.

Chapter Forty-seven

Janie

"You're going to be fine, Janie." The PA nodded to the nurse, who began taking notes. "We'll want to keep her overnight with the monitor in place. I want you to check in on her every few hours. Make sure the heart beat stays up. Watch her blood pressure. Check her fluids. You know the drill."

The nurse smiled at me and patted my arm. "I've been doing this for thirty years. I'm pretty sure I know my way around a pregnant lady."

The PA smiled, and stood to go. "Your baby is stable for the moment, Janie. From your description of the fall you took recently, it's likely all of this has to do with that. You'll stay here tonight, and I'll be back in the morning to check on you. Stay. In. Bed. Okay? You need to be as horizontal as possible. No getting up, for any reason, you hear?"

I nodded, tears welling up in my eyes. "Okay," I managed to whisper. "Thank you."

* * *

I lay as still as possible, willing to connect with the baby inside of me. I wanted to be a good mother. I wanted to take good care of my child. Most of all, I wanted the opportunity to do both of those things.

Thank you, God. I promise, I'll do better. I promise.

A light tap came on the door as it cracked open. Mama, Daddy, and Ms. Ellie tentatively poked their heads in. Daddy smiled, and pushed the door wider.

"It's okay, Daddy. You can come in." I smiled thinking of the many times in my life I'd done the same thing in the middle of a thunderstorm, or a nightmare I couldn't sleep through.

Ellie stepped to my side, leaned over and kissed my head. "I know ya'll need to talk," she whispered. "I just had to see you for myself. Plus, Zee's doctor just messaged me. Good news, I think."

I smiled and nodded. I held onto Ellie's fingers as she pulled her hand away and quietly left the room.

The silence was deafening.

"Mama, Daddy . . ." I tried to form the words. I stopped short and watched them carefully. Could I trust them? Daddy sat on the edge of the bed, his eyes swollen and red. I knew he only had the best in mind for me. Behind him, Mama sat, her eyes cast down. The memory of the clinic flashed through my mind.

Chapter Forty-eight

Charlotte

I entered the room behind David and Ellie, wondering if I should even be allowed to be with my daughter. Janie's tiny body was tucked in beneath the hospital sheets. She seemed so fragile, so small. Tubes hung from behind her that led into her arm. A huge monitor on wheels sat to the left side of the bed, blinking and beeping to the beat of what? It was almost too hard for me to look at.

My only child in such a dangerous state. I'd been too careless with her.

"Mama, Daddy . . ."

I swallowed hard, afraid to hear what I already believed to be true. I pushed the thought of Purdy's backlash behind me. What was done, was done. I'd worry about the gossip tree later.

"I don't really know how to tell you this . . ." Janie closed her eyes. "So, here." She pointed us toward a monitor and leaned to turn it in our direction.

The metal box resembled an ancient television screen, only showing green and black. There were two horizontal rows of lines. The top one larger than the bottom. The top grid showed a series of jagged lines jumping above and below a centered anchor. The bottom grid showed the same but with much smaller, more frequent jumps.

I didn't get it. If she was only a couple of weeks pregnant, how on earth could they find the heartbeat?

"See this?" Janie tried to explain. "This is my heartbeat. It's strong and steady. I'm going to be fine, okay?"

David smiled and took Janie's hand, kissing it gently.

"And, then this. This smaller one. This is . . . your grandchild. Their heartbeat."

David stared oddly at me and blinked hard, shaking his head as if to clear his mixed thoughts and emotions.

"Our?" He tried.

"I know. It's a lot to take in. And, I have some explaining to do. To a lot of people. But, the main thing is, I'm still pregnant. About eleven or twelve weeks, I think."

Eleven weeks? "But, that's impossible, Janie. The . . . clinic. How did . . ." A rush of elation filled my heart. I couldn't comprehend it all. But, the joy was overwhelming. "Did you?"

Janie smiled sheepishly and shook her head no. "I couldn't, Mama. But, I can't say I'm sorry, because I'm not."

"Sorry? I'm the one who's sorry, Janie. I've spent the last weeks regretting every moment we were there. Begging God for another chance—" The words fell on me like an avalanche. I slid off the bed, sunk to my knees, and laid my head on Janie's hand.

Thank you, God. Thank you.

I lifted my head and took Janie's other hand. David came in behind me, beaming. The three of us huddled there, smiling at each other.

"The nurse says they're going to do an ultrasound in the morning before they let me go. If you guys want to be here for that . . . I'd love it." Janie rubbed her stomach. "But, for now, I'm really tired. You don't have to stay. Beside, that chair doesn't look very comfortable."

David laughed and took me around the shoulder, pulling me to him and kissing my forehead. I laughed lightly and the tension of the past weeks seemed to float further from us it as it lifted above the room and away from us all.

* * *

The sun poured into the kitchen, dancing off of the tiny glass window-catcher that read "Grandma". David had insisted we stop in the gift shop as we left the hospital the night before, and had to get it for me. I'd never been so proud.

We were dressed and ready to go at least an hour before we needed to leave the house. A new energy burned between us. One of hope, and forgiveness, and moving forward in a different direction. I took my coffee to the patio, hoping to speed the time.

I sat in my chaise and closed my eyes against the warmth of the sun. I smiled in spite of myself, and let out a laugh.

"Well, my goodness. She's finally snapped." Purdy leaned over me, blocking my light.

"Don't you have a town of little people to drop down on and terrorize?" I replied without opening my eyes.

"Funny, Char. Actually, yes. It's called the church daycare. And, apparently, it's my day to drop off the donations. Want to come?"

"With you? Of course not."

"Oh, pooh. Really? You're going to make me trample through the rug rats on my own?"

"It'll do you good. Besides, there's somewhere I need to be. Janie's still in the hospital, not that you care."

"Well, of course I do. But, I couldn't sit there all night long. I do have a life, you know."

"I know, I know. Like I said . . . the town of little people. Flying monkeys. I get it, Pur." I opened one eye.

Purdy's lips drew into a tight line. "What if I come pick you up afterward? Will you help me then?"

"Fine."

"Fine. I'll see you later."

"Fine." I could get use to this new attitude with my sister. I peeked once more to see Purdy rushing back to her lair.

"It's time," David called out the back door.

I stood up and brushed myself off, ready to meet my grandbaby.

Chapter Forty-nine

Janie

I lay as still as I could with the gooey clear gel being swirled around my stomach.

I giggled. "Sorry," I giggled again. "I'm . . . really ticklish."

The doctor smiled.

Mama and Daddy stood to my left as the doctor worked on my right. The monitor was turned toward them, though I couldn't make out much beyond a static blur. The nurse came in beside the doctor and plugged in something he'd obviously forgotten. A whir-bump, whir-bump, whir-bump sounded over the speaker. She winked at me.

"Is that? Is that its heartbeat?" I asked laughing louder now.

"Yes," the doctor chuckled. "It sounds strong. Good. If you look over here, we can see . . . well, there's the head . . . ten fingers . . . a healthy spine . . . and its heart."

Mama began to cry. She held her hand over her mouth, crying and laughing at once. Daddy's eyes teared up, and he coughed to hold them back. I giggled as my heart soared.

"Well, that is just . . . the most beautiful thing I've ever seen. David, look." Mama pointed toward the screen with one hand and covered her mouth with the other. Tears fell across her hand and when she moved to wipe them away, I couldn't help but smile at the open mouthed grin Mama couldn't contain.

Gabby had been right all along, my prayers were being answered.

Chapter Fifty

Charlotte

I'd spent my morning with the three most amazing people I would ever be blessed to know. The third, I couldn't wait to meet. I kissed David goodbye at the exit door of the hospital and waited a few feet inside for Purdy.

After a few moments, I realized I was supposed to call her when we were done. I pulled out my blackberry, pegged the keys, and sat down prepared to wait a while.

R U COMING OR NOT EVIL?

Within moments, Purdy pulled through the covered drive.

"What were you doing? Hiding out in the bushes over there?"

"No. I just started heading this way and I got your text. Perfect timing, I guess." Purdy looked away, flipping her hair.

"Alright. Let's get this over with so I can get home. There's a nursery I need to start working on." I put on my sunglasses and looked back at the hospital trying to pick out the window of the room that had changed my life.

"So. Spill it. How'd she get knocked up twice in three months?" Purdy asked matter-of-fact as if it was her right to know. She adjusted her rear view mirror as if talking to someone that way was acceptable and common.

I just stared at her and said nothing.

"Okay. I'm sorry. That was harsh. Um . . . how did my precious niece fall into such unfortunate circumstances? It's a terrible shame on me that I couldn't do more to help her. Better?"

"That almost sounded genuine."

"Come on, Charlotte. Fill me in."

"Fine. I'll fill you in. But, when you haul it over to Daddy's and Flora's you'd better get every last detail right. Understand? If I'm going to be disowned, I at least want it to be for the right reasons."

Purdy cocked her head to the side and pulled the car off the road, giving me her full attention. I paused as long as I could stand it, causing her to squirm.

"Janie's still pregnant. She never went through with the abortion. I don't know all the details or how she managed to do it without us knowing, but she didn't have the abortion. The baby—my grandbaby—is three months along."

Purdy's mouth fell open. "Didn't have it?" She snapped her head to stare out the windshield, and then turned back to Charlotte. "How is that even possible? They would have told me. I mean us."

I grinned. "Apparently not."

"Wh—what does that mean? She's still pregnant with the same baby she went to the clinic with?"

"Yes." I was really enjoying dragging this reaction out.

Purdy kept glancing around, with a far off expression on her face. "Charlotte. Are you seriously going to ruin the family over this? You're going to let your unmarried daughter destroy the Parkers over a bastard child?"

Anger surged through my body, but I tried to remain composed. "You'd better watch yourself, Purdy. It's my grandchild regardless of how it got here."

"Oh, well. That makes it all better then. I'll explain that to Daddy sitting in the back of the ambulance, after he's had his stroke. It's because you're a grandmother now. Perfect."

"I don't care what anyone says, Purdy. I saw the baby today. On the monitor. And . . . it was the single most beautiful thing I've ever laid eyes on."

"Oh, give me a break. It's not even a baby yet. Beside, no need to do that whole dance for my benefit. There's still time. In fact, I can call over to the clinic right now—"

"No." I said with a forcefulness I didn't know was in me.

"You can't be serious, Charlotte. Here, let me just . . ." Purdy picked up her cell as I watched her dial information.

I yanked it out of her hand, rolled down the window, and tossed it into the tobacco field beside us.

"What? You can't just decide this, Butterfly. This is a family matter, whether you like it or not. We're going over to Daddy's right now. You're not leaving this on me to share."

I got out of the car, stepping into the sunlight and slammed the door behind me. I wouldn't give them the satisfaction of even thinking they had a say in this.

"Get back in here. Right. Now. Do you hear me? I'm not going over there alone. You're telling them, Charlotte. Right. Now. RIGHT. NOW!" Purdy's eyes were wild, and her head shook from side to side as she screamed at me.

As calm as I could, I said "No, I'm not."

"Yes, you are."

"No, I'm not," I said smiling.

"Charlotte Parker, you get in this car immediately! People will think you've lost your mind roaming the street like this. Get in here now. I'm not taking this to them like some juicy piece of gossip."

"Of course you are, Purdy. It's what you do. And, you can call me Charlotte Johnston, thank you very much." I left in the opposite direction, marching with new purpose as a tattered woman in a fine automobile shouted obscenities at me from her car window.

Chapter Fifty-one

Janie

Incredibly, I'd survived the inquisition by the Parkers. Everyone from my Aunt Flora, to my third cousins Mamie and Martha—every single Parker woman—had cornered me at various moments in the days following the hospital. They all asked the same question: "Do you know what you're doing to us?" They were all of one mind—or one mind washing it seemed, directed by Purdy. Had it not been for Mama's change of heart and fixed determination to make it all work, I might have caved. But together, we couldn't be swayed. And for some reason, Grandpa Parker seemed secretly happy about it.

Ms. Ellie continued to check in on me and I wondered if it was all too hard on her. If thoughts of possibly losing her child while I gained a child were haunting her. But, she seemed to get better with each day, and from the little she would tell me, Zee was improving and might be able to come home soon. As soon as I released by the doctor to resume regular activity, I went straight to Grace House.

I pushed the heavy door open, as if I'd done it every day of my life. I walked into a rush of children moving from one side of the house to the other, Ms. Ellie in their midst.

"Oh, honey. I'm so glad you're here." Ms. Ellie called from the back of the crowd. "I really need an extra hand. Rupert, the cook, is under the weather and I'm trying to get lunch put away and herd them back to class. Do you think you could jump in?"

I nodded laughing, like I had a choice, as a wave of children pushed me through the crowd. A bell rang overhead and the scrambling of feet and chatter of small voices filled the house. I stood in the hall, making sure everyone stayed in lines and that the little ones didn't get trampled. For so many children in one place, everyone was well-behaved. They turned at the slightest sound of my voice and responded quickly to my requests to go this way or that. I wondered if they longed for guidance so much they jumped at the chance to obey direction.

As the last ones filed into rooms, I returned to the front desk and sat down as the chair squeaked. I closed my eyes and took in a deep breath. A dull headache was beginning to grow, and I pulled out my pocketbook to find something to take.

"You got a baby in there?" A small voice whispered from under the desk. Gabe was hiding in the same corner where we'd first met.

"In my pocketbook?" I teased. "Um . . . no."

"No, silly," Gabe giggled. "In your stomach. Is there one?"

My hand drew to my stomach. My other hand still in the pocketbook. I found a bottle of Tylenol and pulled it out. "Yes," I whispered. "Either that, or a watermelon's growing."

He snatched the medicine away and said, "Then you can't have that."

"Hey! My head is killing me." I struggled to get at him under the desk.

"No. No drugs with a baby in your tummy."

I stopped mid-grab.

Gabe's brown eyes pled with concern.

"They're not real drugs, Gabe. Just headache medicine," I tried. He wouldn't budge.

"See? Right here. Not for babies . . ." he pointed to the back of the bottle, his eyebrows bent and lip poking. I wondered if he was even old enough to read it.

I realized what this meant to him and bent down and hugged him. "I would never do anything like that on purpose, Gabe. Thank you."

"They're here! They're here!" A tiny girl screamed as she rushed down the stairs.

Ellie came in from the kitchen, wiping her hands on an old plaid apron, as the kids who'd gone to class began being led by their teachers into the hall. They gathered around the windows and door at a young couple pulling up the drive. The tiny girl twirled in a pink dress, her bobbed brunette hair held in place by a plastic poodle clip. Her blue eyes dazzled as she looked around to her friends, bouncing with each breath.

"Who?—" Janie started.

"Okay, everyone. We're going to use our very best manners with Katie's new parents. No pushing, no yelling, and no . . . crying. This is a happy day for us. We're happy for Katie that she's found a wonderful home. Aren't we?"

A mound of heads bobbed up and down, but never moved their eyes from the beautiful young couple that approached. The young woman, dressed in a pink sun dress was smiling as she glanced through the span of tiny faces waving and pointing at her. Her husband opened the trunk of the car, and then rushed up behind his wife, holding loosely to her back.

Ellie parted the crowd and opened the door. "We've um . . . been expecting you," she laughed.

The couple smiled to each other as the husband shook Ellie's hand.

"I think she's ready," Ellie said, her voice cracking.

"Here! I'm over here!" Katie shouted from the middle of the crowd, her head poking up and down trying to be seen.

"Hello, precious," the man called and reached over the crowd to pick up his new daughter. A flurry of hands reached up to touch him, this mystery thing, this father. My heart ached for them all.

Katie snuggled into his neck, then reached for her new mother. The young woman picked her up as naturally as any mother would, and kissed her on the cheek leaving a pink smear.

"Well, we at Grace House maintain a strict policy about pick-ups. As you know, Katie's had her chance to say goodbye to everyone. You can take a few moments to gather her things by the door, and then it would be best for everyone if you went ahead. If you'd like to come back in a few weeks to check in, that would be . . . lovely." Ellie choked.

Katie dropped from her mother's arms and rushed to Ellie, burying her face. "I love you, Miss Ellie. I love you."

"I love you too, my Katie. So much." She nodded toward the young couple who clung to each other, the woman's hand over her heart. "So, it's time for you to go. But, you'll always, always have a place here, okay? You remember that. Always."

Katie nodded, wiping her eyes. "Oh! I almost forgot!" she squealed and rushed up the stairs. Her steps echoed through the empty hall and soon she was coming back down, carrying something fuzzy and pink. "Mr. Beezer!" she yelled. "I almost forgot Mr. Beezer!"

She rushed to the bottom where her new mother put her hand out to carry her toy. But, Katie hurried past them and into the dining room as the room cleared of children, rushing to follow her. The adults tarried behind.

"Right there! Right there beside that doll!" Katie yelled, jumping up and down.

Ms. Ellie pulled a dining chair near the wall and stood under a long shelf that lined the room about two feet from the ceiling. "These are their pieces," Ellie explained.

The new parents and I eyed each other, confused.

"Each child that leaves us leaves one of these behind. It's a piece of their heart. Something for us to remember them by, and something they know will always be here, when they're ready to come and visit."

Katie's parents nodded and smiled, the young woman started crying. Janie watched as Ellie carefully balanced on the chair, and then lifted on her tiptoes to place the matted pink teddy bear on the shelf.

When she was done, they stood back, and everyone marveled. My breath caught as I recognized the very doll the girl had asked to be beside: Bracey.

As the family moved back towards the front door, a mass of children followed. I felt frozen, unable to take my eyes off Bracey. Had something happened that I was too weak to be told about? Certainly, Mama would have—

"It's not what you think," Miss Ellie came behind me and squeezed my shoulders. "Give me a sec to finish up here, then we'll talk."

I sank into a dining room chair, more relieved than I'd ever been. I laid my head against the back, and closed my eyes.

Please let him be okay.

A noise above me caused my body to jerk and I reopened my eyes to see Bracey flying off the shelf, then slinking across the floor. What on earth? I looked under the table for Gabe, thinking he was trying to get my goat again. But, no one was there. As I sat back up, I almost missed a sway in the curtains. My eyes followed the movement down to the floor where two feet poked beneath the hem.

It only took a second for my mind to put it all together. A snicker from beneath the long length of velvet confirmed it:

Zee was hiding.

Chapter Fifty-two

Charlotte

I slipped on the new raspberry colored dress I'd just bought at Layla's Boutique on Main, and pulled my brown hair into an upward twist, securing it with a diamond studded hair clip. Zirconias, really. I tilted toward the mirror, noting the crow's feet that deepened the edge of my eyes. Laugh lines, I preferred to call them. I dotted my lips with clear gloss, smacked them together, and smiled at myself.

As I drove toward the club that Monday, I felt renewed with energy. A new spring brought with it the joy of warmth after months of cold. I cracked my window a bit, allowing the air to flow across my face but not mess up my hair. The scent of freshly cut grass filled the air. I pulled into the drive, dropped my keys at the valet, and hurried in. I didn't want to miss a thing.

I turned toward my regular table but saw the girls waiting for me at another one, waving me over. I didn't waste a moment, and hurried over to greet them.

"Gammie, we match!" Evie shouted and twirled.

I rushed to her and held her hand as we circled together in sync, one big pink swirl. "We're practically twins," I whispered to my granddaughter, whose eyes lit with the precious idea of it all.

"Mama, Ellie's going to be late today. She just called," Janie said.

"Is everything okay?" I placed my pocketbook on a chair as Evie rifled through it and pulled out a small tube of lip gloss.

"For me?!" Evie squealed.

I winked and smacked my lips together. Evie spread the gloss around her lips, her chin, and nose, smacking with each round. Janie and I busted in giggles.

"That's plenty, Evie," Janie insisted, looking worn and tired with the trials of young motherhood. Raising a three year old on your own was no easy task.

"Oh, let her, Janie. For me."

Janie laughed, shaking her head to oblige.

Evie brought her favorite doll, as she did each week, and it sat in a place of prominence, in the chair beside me. Its dark hair had become matted in the three years since I'd given it to her on the day she was born. An old baby dress of hers had come to replace the original which had been "decorated" with a variety of sharpies one day when Janie wasn't looking. Covering its feet were the tiny pink booties Evie had worn home from the hospital. To me, they represented a reunion of sorts, between my heart and Janie's.

Gabby and her oldest daughter, a pure beauty at the age of twelve, came in smiling at Evie and stood back to admire her. Evie, of course, ate that up and got more dramatic with each set of eyes that paused to notice. Before long, every table within ten feet was smiling and winking at her as she hammed it up twisting, and dancing, and well, doing anything that came to her three year old mind apparently.

"You're cuter than a wink," Gabby said smiling.

"I don't know where on earth she gets that from," Janie said.

But, I had an idea. There was more Parker in her than I cared to admit.

We finally settled into our seats as Ellie rushed in, hand in hand with Zee, and took theirs. Evie watched Janie closely and mimicked every move she made: laying her napkin on her lap, crossing her legs, politely listening without interrupting—well, at least she tried. She had become the single most joyful thing in my life. Just watching her filled me with emotions I can't express. Even in the smallest things. There wasn't a day that went by that I didn't thank God for ruining my plans. I didn't know how I ever lived without her.

We'd been coming to the club every Monday for the last three years. After finding I was going to become a grandma, I decided I needed to make wiser choices in friends and stopped going to the Monday Ladies Lunch. Well, to be honest, Purdy decided for me when David and Daddy agreed it was time to sell the family business, and David began helping me build my dream: The Pink Magnolia, my flower shop. But, I had not planned to return to her nonsense anyway. From what I was told, several new women had been thrilled to replace Maimie and me. I imagined them showing up the first day, dressed to the nines, perfectly coiffed, taking their rightful place in the elite society of Riverton. I wondered how long it took them to realize how empty that place of honor felt, or how instead of opening their horizons, they would soon vehemently protect them.

The waiter came to our table, bringing a pink rose for Evie. "Good morning, ladies. What will we be having today?"

"Sketti!" Evie shouted.

Janie shook her head, "Not with that new dress on, poodle. How about grilled cheese?"

"Cheese! Cheese!" she shouted as if we were at a ballgame instead of a country club. I had to admit, I enjoyed the contrast of it.

"Cheese it is, Miss Evie," the waiter said. "Ladies?"

Each of us went around the table, placing our orders. No one felt pressured to ask for salads they didn't want, or consider calories they didn't need. We ordered what we craved with no fear of judgment. I considered how many Mondays I'd sat in this very room eating raw veggies I despised, while making small talk with women I liked even less.

Just as we finished our orders and the conversation settled down, a loud cackle from the front entrance sent a shiver down my spine. Purdy. Most Mondays we managed to avoid her crowd. But, today, a business luncheon had taken over and we were forced to sit only a few tables away from the standard table Purdy insisted they hold for her each week.

It had been several months since I'd seen her. The years seemed to be wearing her down. Her once precisely placed hair now regularly sprouted rebellious strands that refused to obey. Her shoulders seemed more rounded now, slumped even, as if the load she carried was too heavy for her to bear. Still, she did what she could to handle herself with pride and glided through the dining room, ignoring the other diners as if they were beneath her. I hoped she'd do me the same favor until—

"Poody! Poody!" Evie jumped up and down in her chair, shaking the table and garnering everyone's attention again.

Purdy glanced slowly in our direction, as if something entirely insignificant were suddenly vying for her favor. She smiled slightly and waved at Evie, thinking foolishly it would suffice.

"Poody! Over here! It's me! Over here, Poody!" Evie jumped higher, nearly sending her chair tilting over backwards.

Having continued on her way, she had to backtrack as gracefully as possible, so as not to cause a scene. Evie smiled a wide smile, and continued to jump tiny jumps as she anticipated what Purdy might do.

"Hello, my precious. Having lunch with the hens today, Darlin'?" she whispered.

Janie and Ellie exchanged glances, rolling their eyes.

Evie stared at her as if completely confused. "No, this is my Mommy," she said plain as day.

"Oh, well then. All the more reason for you to sit with Aunt Purdy instead."

Evie shot a look toward Janie, apparently panicked that Purdy might be serious.

"Oh, don't worry, poodle. Mean old Aunt Purdy has no intention of you sitting at her table. It's harder to lie in front of children. They'd have absolutely nothing left to say."

"Cute," Purdy said rolling her eyes. "I'll see you boys later," she called as she began to walk away.

"Poody! No. Nooooo. You sit me," Evie said patting the generous three-inch space she'd allowed for Purdy on her seat cushion.

"Aww. Isn't that cute, Purdy? She hasn't noticed your tail end is the size of Riverton Park yet," I said.

"I won't dignify that remark with a reply, Butterfly. I try to maintain certain decorum around here, if you haven't noticed."

"Oh, we've noticed," Janie said smiling and nodding toward Purdy's table of friends cackling and holding their hands to their mouths over someone's misfortune, for sure.

For a split second, Purdy's face fell. If I hadn't been watching her so closely, I may not have caught it. Her eyes went to the floor and she let out a quick, but solemn, breath. I wondered if she wanted to be with her table at all. Was she trapped in her own web?

"Purdy, we really can pull up another chair if you like," I said. Everyone's head snapped in my direction.

"What? Trade this little mop-head gathering for a day with my friends? No thank you."

"Of course not. Who wouldn't rather be with them? Oh yeah . . . all of us," I said winking at Evie. She ran over to me and climbed onto my lap, lifting her tiny hand to rub Purdy's arm.

It touched her. I saw it in her eyes. The struggle there. The temptation to stay with us. The duty to go to her friends. She paused a moment longer than she should have, then turned toward her usual table, and said, "Stop by and see me later, precious," to Evie.

I watched her walk over to the large flawless gathering that was her table.

As the waiters came and placed our meals before us, lifting the stainless covers to reveal our choices, we paused and gathered hands in our own small circle as Ellie led us in prayer.

I didn't close my eyes at first, but instead glanced at each of my loved ones around the table, mentally touching each head that bowed. I asked God to bless them and thanked Him for teaching me that in letting go, I gained everything.

From a table a few feet away, I caught Purdy's eye. I closed my eyes and began to pray she might let go as well.

About the Author

LAURA FRANCES grew up in the south, residing in North Carolina for most of her life. While she is southern, she is no southern belle. She loves the genuine, authentic people who call the south home, and is constantly inspired by the stories of their lives.

She pulls much of her inspiration from her passion for families and especially the relationship between mothers and their children. She hopes to inspire moms of all kinds to live life to the fullest.

Feel free to contact her. She loves to hear from readers. Email her at laura@laurafrancesauthor.com

For more on Laura, visit
http://www.laurafrancesauthor.com

Left wanting more?

Get Excerpts of Laura's Books for **FREE**

Sign up for Laura Frances' occasional newsletter to receive updates, giveaways, sneak peeks, products, and more!

As a fan, you'll get FREE excerpts of each book Laura releases from Lost Sock Publishing as soon as it's available.

SIGN UP AT:
www.laurafrancesauthor.com

Follow Laura Frances on social media to stay up-to-date with her writing and newest releases.

www.laurafrancesauthor.com

Made in the USA
Las Vegas, NV
07 October 2022